TOUCHED BY FIRE

MAGIC WARS: DEMONS OF NEW CHICAGO

KEL CARPENTER

Touched by Fire

Kel Carpenter

Published by Kel Carpenter

Copyright © 2020, Kel Carpenter LLC

Edited by Analisa Denny

Proofread by Dominique Laura

Proofread by Victory Editing

Cover Art by Covers by Juan

 Created with Vellum

To my past self, we did better when we knew better.
It's okay to let go.

"There is a luxury in self-reproach. When we blame ourselves, we feel that no one else has a right to blame us. It is the confession, not the priest, that gives us absolution."

Oscar Wilde, *The Picture of Dorian Gray*

"Grief is not as heavy as guilt, but it takes more away from you."

Veronica Roth, *Insurgent*

TRENTON MCARTHUR WAS the epitome of a fuck boy. Young, mid-twenties in appearance. More than a little cocky. Arrogant. Solid looks. A warlock of moderate status, and rich as hell.

In another life, he would have been a frat boy from Florida State—had magic not become known to humankind and the entire world upended as a result.

There was just one minor problem with Trenton.

He liked to gamble. A lot. Unfortunately for him, he sucked at it, and he didn't pay his debts. Which is what led us here tonight. Him, to play a few rounds of cards in one of the few places in town that wouldn't kick him out. Me, to nab his ass.

It was Friday, after all. Payday.

With my feet kicked up on the old, dingy tabletop, I waited for him to make his way through the bar.

Leaning back, I flipped my lighter open and closed with the tip of my thumb. It was an old habit. The tiny yellow flame flickered in and out of existence.

Trenton and the bartender made nice, fist bumping and doing some weird handshake thing between them. I knew from his file sitting at home on my desk that he and Egzy Daniels went way back. Egzy was just as deep in shit, if not more so, but the lucky bastard hadn't pissed off the wrong people, and so he was safe where he was. For now.

He and Trenton talked for a while, swapping stories about selling potions to minors and sharing exaggerated details of girls they'd fucked last week. Some werewolf beta named Lizzy apparently got around. I silently questioned her life choices while I watched them settle into a routine of familiarity. After a few minutes of that, Egzy clapped my target on the back and walked him my way.

They stopped before me, and I smiled.

"Hello, boys . . ." I purred, dragging my feet from the tabletop. They hit the floor with a loud smack, and the bar quieted for a second before resuming its bustling activities.

Trenton's eyes scanned my form as I scooted down my seat and came to stand before him. The tight black jeans definitely got his attention, but the long-sleeved turtleneck and leather jacket . . . less so.

"Egzy," he drawled. "Who is this?"

"I'm sorry, man," the bartender said, blowing the ruse. I rolled my eyes, dropping any pleasantness from my face. Trenton only needed a second to realize what was up. His mouth started moving, and being the smart person I was, I pistol whipped him faster than a two-pump chump could get off.

A groan fitting the sound effect for my metaphor slipped from Trenton's lips, and I wrinkled my nose. That saying no longer appealed in any way, shape, or form.

He crumpled to the ground, unconscious for the moment.

"You suck at this," I said to Egzy, who stood across from the body looking uncertain about his role to play.

"Trenton's my boy," the bartender complained. I glared at him, taking in his short black hair and tan skin. His features were what I would have called Asian, at least what I knew of Asia before the world went to shit. After the Magic Wars, it was hard enough to find out about other cities in America, let alone countries and continents around the globe. I had no idea if Asia was still the same, or even called that anymore. There was not much of a way to know, given the collapse of technology and the rise of magic. "I didn't wanna rat on him . . ." He pouted.

While Egzy was sort of attractive and low enough on the magic spectrum that he was almost human, he was also dumb as a box of rocks and mostly got by on luck.

"Yeah, well, the deal was that you help me get him out of here without a struggle. My boss isn't going to be happy," I said, lying through my teeth. Egzy didn't know who my boss even was, or that they didn't give two shits if I captured him or not. They only wanted Trenton for the time being. Dealing with dumb criminals had its benefits.

Sometimes.

"You don't think he's going to send someone after me, do you?" Egzy asked, panic flaring in his face. I shrugged.

"I don't know, but maybe you should have thought of that before you tipped off your boy Trenton here," I said, motioning to the unconscious douchebag sprawled out on the floor.

Egzy looked from his prone friend and back to me, then grimaced. He turned on his heel and bolted through the back door while I stood there shaking my head.

Typical. Fucking typical.

This was exactly why I worked alone nowadays. Trenton just happened to be a high-profile client that needed some semblance of discretion. So much for that. As I bent to grab him by the collar of his shirt, I noticed half the bar behind me had stood up.

Goddamn supernaturals.

Always with the pack mentality.

They could fight among each other like dogs, but when a human entered the mix, it was us versus them.

"What are you doing?" Crouched over, I peered between my legs at the big burly man and cursed. He was probably a shifter, and an alpha, given the assertiveness. Betas were more my style. Omegas didn't bother with shit unless there was literally no other choice.

I straightened my back and gazed over at him.

"Mind your own business, buddy," I said. "You don't want to get involved."

He stepped forward. "Actually, I think I do." Yup, my initial guess was right. Definitely an alpha. Standing behind him was probably a group of betas. Not to mention the other supes in the bar. I let out a ragged breath. My heart started to speed up.

I didn't panic. Not like most humans.

When confronted with conflict, I got this giddy excitement inside. It was crazy, and extremely self-destructive, but all my life I'd found myself unable to back down from a fight if directly faced with one.

"I got a bone to pick with this guy," I said, nudging Trenton with my boot.

"Really?" the alpha said, taking another step forward. "Because it looks like you're a hunter, and I don't like hunters."

I lifted both hands in surrender, though one of

them was holding a firearm, so I doubted it looked as innocent as I'd hoped. "I'm not with human patrol," I said, and for once I was telling the truth. What I didn't say was that I used to be. It was how I got my start. "This isn't a speciesist thing."

"Who's your boss?" the alpha asked, and I knew this was going to go one of two ways.

I could tell them who I worked for, and there would be good odds everyone would sit the fuck down. But my boss didn't exactly like being known. He liked it even less when his employees used his name to get out of trouble. Wasn't good for business.

If I told them who, and he found out—which he would—I'd be fired within twenty-four hours as the best-case scenario. Worst-case, he'd take it personally and my head would come off.

Which meant plan B.

I groaned.

"Why couldn't Egzy do the *one* thing," I complained. Using my foot, I kicked the unconscious dude in the side, and he went sliding under the table I'd been seated at. In a single motion, I cocked my gun and fired.

The bullet landed between the alpha's eyes. The skin around the edges glowed orange and sizzled. He fell backwards, hitting the floor with a loud thud.

The sound seemed to spur the bar into motion. All at once, half of it tried to flee and the other half decided to stand their ground. I ran, sliding over the bar top and flipping over the other side to land on my ass and hide behind it. I pulled the second pistol from my jacket, turned, and peered over the edge.

Supes mowed over one another to get to me and I opened fire.

Gunshots went off left and right, loud enough to only add to the pandemonium. Bullet casings hit the veneered counter with little *tinks*. I shot one after another, aiming for the same place each time.

The fun thing about supes was that for a long time they were really fucking hard to kill.

Each of them had different weaknesses, and most of them were nothing like the legends.

Vampires, while they didn't like sunlight, they didn't burn alive in it. It just blinded them.

Werewolves weren't allergic to silver. At all. In fact, no metal really harms them. It's where you hit them that matters.

Witches and warlocks would be the easiest, were they not such a pain in the ass to get near. A single word or wiggle of their fingers and they could kill you faster than you could kill them.

And that was really just the tip of the iceberg as far as supernatural species went.

The one thing I really had going for me was that I was a near-expert on all of them.

Being human and only a little kid when magic

became known in the world had its perks. Largely that I had the time to study them, because in a world where half the people had magic and weren't afraid to use it—being human was a major disadvantage.

So I embraced the one universal truth I knew: knowledge is power.

And because of that, I knew a single shot between the eyes would either kill or disable everyone in this bar. The best part? They usually woke up with jumbled memories from their brain healing and didn't remember me shooting them.

The click of my guns trying to fire and failing to release jarred me back to the moment.

"Shit," I cursed under my breath.

The time it took me to pull a magazine from my jacket cost me. I exhaled harshly as some vampire bitch came flying at me with fangs snapping.

My back hit the concrete floor behind me as she straddled my body. Her pale, sallow cheeks and violet eyes told me she hadn't fed recently enough. She pinned me as I focused on releasing the empty magazine and shoving the new clip in it. Just as it clicked, she loomed only inches from my face.

"You're a feisty one," she purred. "I'm going to enjoy this."

Her jaws stretched wide as her eyes zeroed in on my neck. The thirst had her in its grips, and I used that to my benefit, letting her lunge for a bite—only to find herself with a mouthful of gunmetal.

I shoved the barrel deep enough down her throat that she gagged. Her fangs bit into the side of my hand, and shock permeated her features before her eyes rolled back in her head. Disgust filled me as I pulled the trigger and the backside of her skull exploded.

The body slumped over me, and I twisted, flinging it away. One of her fangs stuck in my hand and I picked it out, flicking it behind my shoulder as I got to my feet.

The bar was silent, everyone in it dead or gone.

Just the way I liked it.

I whistled to myself as I went to grab Trenton.

He was just starting to stir as I dragged him from under the table.

Perfect timing.

2

"Wh—what's going on?" Trenton asked, jerking awake. I was surprised it took him so long to come to, in all honesty. "Who are you?" he demanded next, jerking at the duct tape I'd used to bind his hands together in front of him. I even taped the fingers together so that he couldn't use them. Most witches couldn't, but it never hurt to be careful.

"Doesn't matter," I said, putting both my hands on the table in front of me. In one of them, I held my gun loosely pointed in his direction. He pulled at the bonds again, quickly realizing I hadn't bothered with his mouth or feet. Time was of the essence at the moment, and I'd done a fast job and then put him in the booth across from me. "I'll have you know that if you try to curse me or use magic, I'll put a bullet in your brain faster than you can complete that spell.

Your friends tried to save you thinking my shot wasn't that good." I motioned to the dead supes around the bar. He took one look and swallowed hard. "They're now dead, and the person who hired me doesn't care if that's the way I bring you in. So, let's have a little chat, then we'll be on our way, and you won't have to see me ever again."

He looked back and forth between me and the dead supernaturals twice before nodding.

"Can I ask who hired—"

"Nope," I interrupted. "You'll find out soon enough, anyway." I smiled, and it was all for my own benefit. Once, I might have felt pity about my actions. That day was almost a decade ago, though, and a lot had happened since then. "Now, tell me what you know about magical comas."

He blinked twice, clearly not expecting that line of questioning.

"Magical comas?" he repeated. I nodded. "Uh, well, a spell has to be cast to be put in one . . ." he started, and I rolled my eyes.

"Yeah, I got that part, Florida State."

"My name is Trenton."

"I'm aware."

We stared at each other for a second before he continued. "There's a number of ways to put someone in a coma using magic. You can be direct and put them in a coma, you can put them in an

11

extended sleep for as long as you want, you can transport their consciousness somewhere else——"

"There's a lot of options," I said. "I know they depend on how powerful or skilled the witch or warlock is. How do you break someone out of one?" This was a conversation I'd had over a hundred times now, and I could already tell it would be the same as all the others.

"The original caster has to do it," Trenton said.

"And if you don't have the original caster?" I asked.

He mulled that over for a moment. "It's near impossible. You'd need to——"

"Assess the cause, figure out the exact spell, find a witch or warlock that basically has the power of a god and can counter it——and then hope that they do it right because if even one thing goes wrong the person in the coma is likely to die. Anything else? Come on, Florida State, dig deep."

His mouth fell open, and then closed. "If you already know all of this, then why are you asking me?" I looked at him and laughed humorlessly.

"Because I keep hoping I'll find someone that can give me a different answer."

At that, I moved to get to my feet.

"What——" he started. I reached over the table and hit him upside the head with the butt of my pistol. Again.

I'd done this exact thing so many times now that just like his answers, I knew where it was going. I'd pull him out of the booth. He'd try to curse me and run. Or, provided we got past that, we'd get out to the street where he would inevitably find some stupid supe that would try to help because they didn't know what they were getting involved with.

Trenton fell sideways, and I hauled him out of his seat. Flinging his longer arm over my shoulder, I wrapped mine around his waist and walked right out the front door.

Now, anyone that saw us would think he was drunk, and I was the poor girlfriend or friend helping his ass get home. Worked like a charm every time.

With it being dark out, most people didn't look close enough to notice how hard I gripped his middle, or that there was a goose egg forming on the side of his head where I'd hit him twice.

The wind whipped through the alleyway the second I made it outside. My blond hair tangled, strands slipping from the braid to cut across my eyes, and they got stuck on my mouth.

"Ugh," I groaned, swiping it back in place once more as I dragged Trenton down the alley with me, thankful for the extra hours I'd been working out. Dark clouds blotted out most of the sky, but an almost full moon peaked through every now and then as the wind blew them south.

Most of the buildings appeared uninhabited, but they would any time after dark, regardless of whether people were in them or not. Not a lot of cars ran in the city nowadays, apart from taxis. They were still heinously expensive, though, and other methods had popped up for getting around, both more and less effective—all relying on magic. I preferred my own two feet because I was the only thing I could trust in this whole goddamned city.

We passed through the worst of town with nothing more than some interested looks from beggars and lowlifes. One flash of my gun and they would turn the other way.

Magic may be flashy and get you far in this world, but a gun still did the trick—less impressive as it may be.

My fingers were stiff, and my cheeks flushed when I finally came to stand beneath the flashing yellow sign that read: The Underworld.

It was a casino, a hotel, a place to buy and sell almost anything—but most importantly, it was where I worked. I walked around the side. The alley was seedy. The pipes leaked. The concrete cracked or was crushed in places. A chain-link fence blocked off the other side, but lucky for me, I only needed the heavy metal door on my right.

I wrenched it open, pushing Trenton through it first, and then following after.

The door slammed shut at my back as lights flickered on in the hallway. At the very end of it, a door that led out into the main casino opened and closed, music played, and lights pulsed with every movement as servers and armed guards walked in and out. I ignored that one for the moment and instead dragged my ass to the door on the right and pounded my fist twice.

Metal creaked. The door opened. Smoke poured out, and the scent of a cigar made my nose wrinkle. I waved a hand in front of my face.

"How's it shaking, Pip?" Ronny said, the cigar hanging out of the corner of his mouth. "This the one?"

"Yup," I answered, giving the unconscious warlock a shove through the door. Ronny was mostly human, and like most low-level supes, he'd always just thought he was blessed with more strength and speed than most people. Then magic became known to the world, and scientists found a way to test if people had any. It was one hell of a shock to find out about half the population was some sort of supe, whether full blood or watered down. In Ronny's case, his grandma tangled with a werewolf, and while he hadn't shifted, he had distinct advancements that weren't human qualities. Like the ability to grab Trenton by the back of the neck and pick him up with one hand.

"Uh—what's going—"

Ronny punched him in the middle, and the wind left his lungs. Trenton groaned loudly, and I rolled my eyes.

"I got it from here," the glorified brute said with a grin.

"Knock yourself out," I muttered, turning from the door as it slammed shut behind me. I walked to the end of the hall and took the door into the casino.

Blue and yellow lights from slot machines went off. I strolled right past them and through the card tables without a second glance. On the far back wall, the bar was up and running. A fairy dressed like she'd just walked out of a porno staged for the 1920s sang a jazzy tune that made my ears want to bleed. Her iridescent wings fluttered, and speckles of gold dust dropped onto the patrons. A subtle abuse of magic if there was one. Her singing sucked ass, but the effects of faerie dust, even in limited quantities, were such a potent aphrodisiac they basically handed her their wallets as she sauntered on by.

I took a seat at the two-person table furthest away from the horrid fairy.

The guy across from me looked up and lifted both eyebrows. His brown eyes widened.

"You already caught him?" he asked, closing the file in front of him. I nodded once, and he picked up his phone. One press of the button and a picture of

Trenton filled the screen. He was being dangled upside down by his feet and beaten to a pulp.

Not an ounce of remorse touched me as I looked from the picture to Anders' face.

He let out a low whistle. "You're a cold-hearted woman, Pip." Then he grinned and winked. "Just the way I like ya."

If Anders wasn't forty with thinning hair and watery blue eyes, I might have found it creepy. As it was, he was human—just like me—and one of the closest things I had to a friend—or he would be, if not for my trust issues.

I pulled my wallet from my back pocket and dropped it on the table. The metal piece hit with a clang that was drowned out by the rest of the casino. "I expect to see the full amount on that screen before I walk out the door," I said, tapping the tiny plastic display, whose row of numbers were awfully close to zero. Wallets in the modern day were all electronic because the potential for magical abuse was too great. It all came in and out of the same bank, and any magic user or hacker dumb enough to attempt to break into it found themselves cursed six ways to Sunday.

"Yeah, yeah," Anders sighed, pulling out his own wallet. He typed in the amount and the end of his turned red. I picked up mine and we touched the ends together, pressing the thumb sensor at the same time.

Both ends flashed green, signaling the transfer went through. I pulled it back and glanced at the number before shoving it back in my pocket.

While my paycheck was no small sum, living in New Chicago wasn't cheap. Not if you wanted electricity, running water that wouldn't give you lead poisoning, and food that didn't come from a factory that stopped producing fifteen years ago when the Magic Wars really dialed up. Even shitty processed food was astronomically priced these days. And fresh stuff? Forget it. If you weren't rich—which humans never were—it was impossible to come by.

"Do you have any other jobs?" I asked.

Anders sighed. "Not witches or warlocks."

My lips pressed together. While I preferred to hunt those that might be of use, I couldn't always afford to be picky. Literally. "What's the most expensive one you have?"

He reopened the file he'd been looking at and scanned it over.

"Human. Pair of them. They decided to pull a little Bonnie and Clyde act stealing from one of the boss's warehouses. Two grand if they're brought in hot. Fifteen hundred cold."

I cursed under my breath. "Two grand?" I repeated. "These days that's barely enough to keep my lights on for a week, Anders."

"I don't make the jobs or decide their worth, Pip.

I'm just the middleman. You know that," he said, pulling a cigarette from his jacket pocket. He snapped his fingers once, and the tip of his thumb caught fire for a brief second, just long enough to light the end.

I rolled my eyes.

"How much did that parlor trick cost you?"

Anders inhaled deeply before exhaling in one smooth stream of smoke. He grinned. "Three days off my life."

I stared at him, shaking my head. "Doesn't that shit kill you fast enough as it is?"

Anders snorted. "Coming from the bounty hunter with the highest kill rate on the job. What is it that you do so differently that you leave a trail of bodies a mile long in your wake?" He pulled over the crystalline tray from the side of the table and flicked the end of the cigarette. Ash dropped into it, disappearing instantly because freakin' magic. "Isn't the job dangerous enough? One might think you're looking to get hurt," he mused.

I groaned. "Piss off. I get the hint."

He winked in good nature, not at all bothered by my words.

"We live in a world where magic exists. Some of us like it for the ease. Some like the novelty. Others like the power . . ." He trailed off. "But not you." He tilted his head, as if thinking about that. "Why is that?"

I leaned back, my gaze sweeping over the casino floor and falling on the jazzy fairy once more. "All magic has a price," I found myself saying softly. "Some of us don't want to pay it."

He looked thoughtful for a moment as he took another huff of smoke.

"Fair enough," he said on his exhale. "The reason you don't want to pay it have anything to do with the witches and warlocks you interrogate before Ronny gets ahold of them?"

I kept my face neutral, not giving a thing away as I replied, "The reason you spend your Friday nights here have anything to do with the picture in your left back pocket? You haven't changed it in the three years I've been working with you. You don't talk about him."

The 'him' in question was the face of a little boy, no older than seven or eight. While grainy, he had the same eyes and weak chin as the man sitting before me. The picture never changed. Never updated. I could be wrong, but I had a feeling I wasn't.

Anders' face lost all of its amusement for a moment as surprise overcame him. He hid it quickly, but I still saw. "You don't miss much, do you?"

"When you got a kill rate as high as mine, you can't afford to," I replied with a tight smile. Anders let out a laugh, taking a swig from his glass of water.

"No, you damn well can't." He took another drag

of his cigarette and I moved to stand.

"It's a pleasure doing business with you—" I started, getting ready to head out.

"Wait," he said, letting out a sigh. "I don't have a bounty per se, but there is something that might be of interest to you."

I settled back in my seat and lifted an eyebrow. "I'm listening."

"We got word recently of a coven planning to attempt a demon summoning," Anders said, lowering his voice to a hush. A chill ran through me. "I don't think I have to tell you how exponentially stupid that is."

"Do they have enough power to succeed?" I asked, running the tip of my finger along the edge of one of the folders.

"To summon it? Yes. To control it? Absolutely not." He looked away and shook his head.

Demon summonings were rare. It took a strong coven to call it, and a near-invincible one to control it. Or so the theory went. No summoning had ever been successful. Every single one documented had ended with the members of the coven slaughtered, and that was the best-case scenario.

Worst-case, they accidentally set it loose on our world.

"What exactly is this job?" I asked Anders.

He leaned back, clearly uncomfortable with what

he was going to say. Little did he know, I already had a strong suspicion and was willing to do it.

"The boss has decided it's in everyone's best interest that the summoning isn't completed. He'd like a message sent to the public about attempting this in his city."

I smiled without happiness. "He wants an execution."

Anders nodded. "This isn't like your usual jobs. The coven is strong, and from what our sources say, they're expecting it—"

"How much?"

He blinked, taken aback. "What?"

"How much are you paying?"

I'd known him a long time. Longer than most, given I wasn't big on making friends when everyone was just looking to climb over you to help themselves. He didn't ask a lot of questions. What he did piece together, he used discretion about. He didn't scare easily. The slight flicker of fear I saw in his eyes in that moment—that was new.

"Five hundred thousand," he said eventually. The look of regret was fleeting, but it was there. I could see why he hesitated.

He could have asked me to kill the demon itself. I was just desperate enough I might have taken it. But an entire coven?

"Consider it done."

3

I STOOD outside the cathedral as the sun went down, painting the sky in red and violet. The wind howled like a ghoul on the hunt. I lifted the collar of my trench coat and stuffed my hands in my pockets. The cheap material did little for my numb fingers, but it was better than nothing. The damned really did have a sick sense of humor, summoning a demon in this kind of place. I shook my head and started down the street, taking the long way around.

In an hour or two, the cathedral would close, and when it did, anyone that was here to pray to whatever god they worshipped would be turned out on the streets. The front doors would lock, and the keys would be handed off to the Antares Coven.

I turned the corner at the end of the street, going down the next block, and coming behind to the back of the cathedral. They would check the pews, probably every room, maybe even the bathrooms, before starting.

Odds were, they wouldn't check the closet holding the extra vestments.

That's exactly where I would be.

I turned down the narrow alley right behind it and followed the pavement to the back. Up three concrete steps was the door I needed. There was only one problem.

It was locked.

Twenty years ago, they might not have locked the door at all. But the world was a different place now, one where it was stupid to walk around unarmed, or in this case, leave anywhere you gave a shit about unlocked. It wouldn't stop supernaturals, but the desperate humans—and there were plenty of them— would have an extra hurdle if they wanted to break in.

Fortunately for me, they were holding it in a church, not a bank. I came prepared.

I pulled out my lock picking kit. Fifteen seconds was all it took to pop.

I stowed the tools back in my jacket and tied the band around my waist once more, holding it closed.

My cold fingers grabbed the colder metal handle. Dried and peeling paint flaked against my fingers as I pulled it open. A warm burst of air hit me, and I quickly stepped inside, closing the door softly behind me. I made a quick beeline down the hall, toward the stairs. Music chased me, the sound of haunting hymns like a hound on my heels, reminding me of another time as I quickly found the closet I needed and pulled the door open.

"Shit," I muttered.

The floor plan for this place hadn't been easy to find, but so far it had been accurate. What it conveniently left off was the dimensions. The closet couldn't have been more than two feet deep and two feet wide. If anyone opened the door, I'd be discovered early and that wouldn't do.

I bit the inside of my cheek, looking down the hall one way, then the other.

Chancing my luck of finding someone, I took the stairs, opting to go up instead of back where I came from.

Maybe . . . a thought came to me, sudden and unbidden.

I followed the stairs up and quickly crossed the ten-foot platform before a second set of stairs. Off to one side, mass was going on, but I stuck to the shadows so they couldn't see me. This second level went around the chapel, branching off into different hallways. I looked down each, periodically peering back over the railing to the congregation below.

When I saw the bright red letters of an exit sign, one corner of my lips tugged up.

I took that hallway, ignoring the doors on either side until I reached the end. It was all metal, painted a soft gray some time ago, but faded and wearing thin in places. I tried the handle, and it gave way.

I slipped out into a stairway that went up and down. Taking my chances that luck would still be with me, I went two more floors where it finally ended. Quickly picking the lock, I popped my head in to see where this had landed me.

Wind caught the ends of my braid, flinging it around. I stepped out onto the roof, not bothering with the spires on either side, and instead moving toward the center where a giant, stained glass ceiling looked straight down to where this summoning would be happening.

"Perfect," I said, quickly getting back in the stairwell to wait out the next few hours.

I leaned back against the brick wall, sliding down to the ground. My head tilted back as the cold seeped in, but without the wind, it was doable. I counted the bricks on the ceiling, moving to the ones on the walls when the stairwell opened again.

"Anyone in here?" a voice that teetered on the line of masculine called. He sounded young, not like a child, but like a boy that was only just becoming a man.

I stayed quiet, opting not to respond and see what he did. A few seconds later the door slammed shut, and all was silent again.

It was almost time. If the Antares Coven were running their checks now, it wouldn't be long. I waited another stretch of counting bricks before rolling to my side. My joints popped as I climbed to my feet and stretched my arms and legs. After hours of sitting in the dark stairwell, my muscles protested the movement almost as much as the stillness. I cracked my neck and opened the door leading out onto the roof.

Night had fallen in the windy city.

A gust hit me full in the face, making my chest tight.

Fucking wind. Fucking cold. I hated them both.

Gritting my teeth, I closed the door as softly as I could, and navigated the dark roof to where the stained glass was now the secondary source of light to the full moon overhead.

"Supernaturals and their moons," I muttered, shaking my head. Any sound I made was lost in the shrieking of the turbulent night skies. I reached back and tucked my braid beneath the collar of my coat to stop it from whipping around everywhere.

The light coming from the glass ceiling brightened, and I moved right to the edge, then peered over it.

It was hard to make out every distinctive detail.

There were four bright globs that I assumed to be fire. One stationed north, south, east, and west—equal distance from each other.

This is where, if I were planning to kill the coven, I should have done so.

I had a better plan, though. One that ended with them dead, me with my money, and perhaps, if I was lucky, my answers too.

I kneeled down, squinting through a single red-stained pane. It was easier to make out the members of the coven then. All thirteen of them wore dark robes, making them indistinct from one another. There was something else . . . something I hadn't seen or planned for.

I squinted, getting so close to the glass that my nose touched.

My eyes widened when I realized what I was looking at.

There in the center of a circle was a person.

I'd bet my right arm, a young girl.

Someone easily manipulated. Someone not quite innocent, but ignorant in how dark the world could be. Someone that was meant to be an offering to the demon they were summoning.

The Antares Coven were bigger idiots than I'd realized.

I jumped to my feet, debating my options.

The first orb of fire went out. *Shit.*

I'd mistimed this. If I took the stairwell, it would be too late. Anyone not in the circle when it was cast wouldn't be able to enter it. Which only left one option.

I stepped back and loosed the tie on my trench coat, quickly reaching for one of my guns. I pointed at the ceiling and hoped like hell that this plan wouldn't kill me. I opened fire. The glass cracked. Pieces fell away as I shot in a wide circle. The only thing worse than what I planned to do was getting stabbed while doing it.

The second orb of fire winked out.

My backpack barely touched the stone roof before I ripped it open and pulled out a grappling hook attached to forty feet of rope. I kept one on me for most missions, just for moments like this. Grabbing the end of the rope, I pulled, and it all unfurled.

The third orb blinked out, the glow from below now muted.

In a single motion, I turned and hurled the hook over the edge of the cathedral.

I couldn't wait for the light to go out completely. If that happened, it was all over. Without checking to see if the hook caught, I took a deep breath.

Then I jumped.

4

My coat flapped in the wind as I rushed toward the ground.

The screams of the night sky didn't fade so much as it was replaced by the ominous chanting of the Antares Coven.

Thirteen members spoke in ancient Hebrew, a language I was uncomfortably familiar with. A chill ran through me right as my left arm pulled taut. The burn in my shoulder as the muscle stretched too far to stop my impact was minor compared to the jarring sensation of being suspended twenty feet above the circle.

I'm going to pay for this later. It was my only thought before I let go entirely.

I bent my knees and rolled when I hit the ground, thankful for my jacket when I felt the small shards of glass press into it.

A less experienced coven would have stopped. If they were lesser prepared, they would have run. These weren't amateurs, though, and my arrival didn't scare them in the slightest.

I looked around the circle at each hooded figure. I couldn't see their faces, but I could see they held athames. Their palms were already cut. Blood dripped from their self-inflicted wounds.

Those scarlet drops splattered the marble floor as their chanting reached its crescendo.

One long note filled the cathedral. Like a battering ram to my memories, it shattered every coherent thought.

Pressure built as magic from another plane flooded the circle. It filled me just as it filled the girl, not yet a woman, who sat on her knees across from me. They'd dressed her in white. She was supposed to bow like the little lamb led to the slaughter. Instead, she'd watched me jump. She saw me land. Our eyes locked as the magic entering this world intensified.

Pain filled her features. Pain and a sudden terrible understanding, as if she only just pieced together why she was actually here. A coven of thirteen could summon a demon with their combined power, but it would drain them, and they needed a funnel. She would get the worst of it.

Under normal circumstances, the sacrifice always died.

Maybe she wouldn't, though. Maybe my presence would be enough.

Light gathered in the center of the circle. Embers of red and orange grew, swirling around each other faster and faster.

There was no way to brace myself for what was coming. I knew it in my bones.

The magic released in a wave of blinding light.

It rolled through me, and I noted the lack of pain only a moment before she began screaming.

Steeped in shadow, a naked figure knelt in the circle where before there had been only light.

Cold rolled through the cathedral as the demon lifted its head.

I could not see its face. Only strong shoulders and dark hair, but I knew it was male by its sheer size.

The screams of the girl quieted. Uneasiness settled in my gut, followed by dread. I hoped I was wrong. I hoped—

"Who is it that calls to me?" His voice was deep as the ocean and expansive as the sky. It was dark and deceptively soft, yet . . . enticing.

A shudder ran through me.

"We have," another voice said. One of the robed forms stepped forward and lowered his hood. He had light brown hair that was thinning into a widow's peak and flat brown eyes. His chin was too pointed to be attractive. His skin was drawn tight in certain places and hung flaccid in others.

He was old and ugly and . . . he hadn't aged a day in the ten years that had passed.

My lips parted as shock ran through me.

My heart pounded in overdrive.

It was him. Claude Lewis. The warlock who could fix *her*. If I could somehow capture him and—

The demon stood and my mouth went dry. All this time the solution to my problem had been right under my nose in this same city. Now that I'd found it, though, I had bigger problems to contend with than the idiot who should have known better than to try this after the first time.

The demon had to be over six feet tall and built of solid muscle. The shadows still clung to him, but I could see through them, taking in the contour of muscle and the markings that lined his arms and shoulders and back. They looked like tattoos, but I knew better.

A demon wore their name upon their body. Their true name.

It encompassed all that they were: magic, soul, and flesh—and it was completely unreadable to humans, or anyone for that matter, apart from other demons.

"You opened the door," the demon said, tilting his

head. Then, slowly, he turned his cheek. One side of his full mouth curved up in an inhuman smile. "But you are not the one that calls." He turned around, and my eyes dropped to the ground just beyond him, to the girl.

She laid with her arms sprawled. Dark hair swept to one side, her face was turned at just enough of an angle that I could see her expression.

The glassy-eyed look was hollow. Any sign of life gone.

I swallowed.

Dead.

She was dead.

The magic to summon and contain the demon in their circle had eaten entirely through her and somehow not harmed me. Had neither of us been there, it would have taken its toll on the coven. As it was, we were—and it hadn't made a damn difference in keeping her alive.

That realization settled around me. If I'd killed the coven as I'd been hired to do, she might have actually lived.

I didn't, and her death would follow me to the grave.

Few did, even after years of killing. But this one would.

This one was personal.

My fingers felt numb around the handle of the

gun. I slowly raised my gaze from the dead teen to the demon in front of me.

Eyes the color of steel and winter nights stared back.

Cold. So cold.

My chest squeezed as my breath caught in my throat. He was the most beautiful and terrifying thing I'd ever seen. The sharp angles of his face were savage. His physical form was perfection, but it was those eyes that told the truth of what he was. The beast beneath the man shone in them.

"We humbly offer this sacrifice as payment—" the man started. His voice harsh and grating.

"Silence, human," the demon commanded. It only served to rile the coven leader further.

"We have summoned you, creature of the night, being of sin and shadows. You are ours to command!" He raised his voice toward the end, and yet the demon didn't react.

I wasn't shocked by his lack of subservience. While the knowledge was almost nonexistent, I knew that summoning didn't actually gain a coven control of the creature they brought to the world. That's part of what made it so dangerous.

That and the fact that the magic they used to call them forth nearly burned every member to their source. They could barely complete the actual summoning, let alone what it would take to truly bind a creature from beyond.

The demon regarded me, turning its full attention my way.

The thing that surprised me was its total lack of reaction. There was no anger. No wrath. If anything, he seemed not to care at all what the coven leader said.

He was too busy staring at me.

"You," he said softly, in that voice of night. "It is you."

"What is me?" I asked him. The words came out softer than I'd intended. His nostrils flared as he took a step in my direction, not even sparing Claude Lewis a glance.

"You are the one that called." He took another step, and my very tiny sense of self-preservation kicked in. I stepped back. The demon narrowed his eyes.

This wasn't supposed to happen.

Not like this, anyway.

They were supposed to summon it, and I would bargain for information. If I were lucky, the creature would turn on them. If not, I had enough bullets.

But *this* . . . this heat, this pounding . . .

This wasn't supposed to be here.

But neither was Claude Lewis.

I'd come here willing to do anything for an answer, and I'd been presented with two.

That stumped me. Without bargaining with the demon, I had little chance of walking away. I needed him on my side, even if it were only long enough to shoot and run.

"I wish to bargain," I managed to say, thankful that my voice sounded stronger—surer than I felt.

"Bargain?" he repeated. Not like he didn't understand the word, but like he didn't understand what place it had here. Which was crazy because bargains were the only way that a summoning could even work. Not that one ever had.

"For freedom," I said, a plan developing in my mind. "And . . ."

"And?" the demon prompted, taking a step closer. A chilled brush of *something* ran up my spine, leaving a trail of gooseflesh in its wake.

"I want you to kill them," I said. My words were met by a cry of protest from those around the circle. While they were not in it, they were also bound to it. If even a single one ran, the circle would break, and with it, any hold they had in keeping us there. I half hoped they would. It would make it that much easier. "That one lives." I pointed to Claude without looking at him.

The corners of his lips lifted slightly, but it wasn't

a kind expression. It was amused, if not a little cruel. "Is that all?" he asked, stepping forward once more.

"Yes," I said.

I was making a deal with a devil. Quite literally.

If I didn't make a deal, though . . . the consequences would be worse. I couldn't die. Not yet. Not before I fixed her.

The demon took another step forward, coming to stand directly before me.

"Very well," he said, softly. "I will bargain with you." I wished I could say that I was relieved, but had I known that Claude would be here, I never would have let them summon a demon. For what demons gave, they asked so much more.

And this demon? I had a feeling he'd demand more than any of them.

"What is the price?" I asked him.

He smiled, and it was tragically alluring. Beautiful and awful at once.

My heart skipped as he leaned forward, our faces only inches apart.

The silver in his eyes was anything but human. It swirled around the dark pupils like mercury. Unnatural and deadly.

I had a feeling in the pit of my stomach what he would ask in return. That didn't make it any easier to hear.

"You."

5

M E.

He wanted me.

My head pounded with the beat of drums. Of battles. Adrenaline flooded my system and my skin became sensitive. Even the brush of air against it felt sharp. Painful. My breath turned ragged.

"You want me?" I asked because my thoughts were scrambled. I needed to buy time.

I could have sworn I saw amusement in his eyes as he said, "I did not stutter."

"Why do you want me?" I replied, a harder tone entering my voice. The amusement that twinkled slowly bled out as something else took its place. Something dangerous.

"Does it matter?" he replied.

"Yes."

"You called to me," he said slowly. "I am intrigued."

"Intrigued?" I repeated.

Slowly, I edged to the side, taking a single step. Black fire raged in his eyes as I did so. Faster than I could react, his hand locked around my wrist, the one not holding the gun.

A jolt like electricity shot through me.

My heart quickened. I sensed my defenses falling. I was approaching that dangerous precipice where there was no coming back.

I couldn't let that happen. For a decade, I'd kept my secret from the world.

It would be another decade before I would let anyone reveal it.

"That's unfortunate," I said softly, my voice mirroring his own. I mimicked the tone intentionally. Even as my heart rate approached that treacherous line.

"How so?" he asked me, clearly perplexed by my words.

The corners of my lips turned up. I lifted the free hand with my gun and pointed it between his eyes. "You can't have me."

Fury flashed through his features. The corded muscle in his neck went taut. The demon's nostrils flared, and I felt the hand locked on my wrist tighten.

Then I pulled the trigger.

A single shot echoed throughout the cathedral.

The hand gripping me slipped, and I darted to the side. While my knowledge of most of the supernatural world was good, demons were in a league all their own. They didn't originate in this world, and there were so few of them that information about them was scarce. I had no idea if that bullet would put him down, or—if it would—for how long.

Magic pulsed within the circle, and it had nothing to do with the coven.

I turned and fired my gun at the witch closest to me.

Red splattered the dais steps as she fell to her knees and toppled sideways. Her athame clattered to the ground. The circle broke.

Cloaked figures ran, sensing their inevitable end.

I popped off two shots and killed the two closest to me that were running toward the side door.

There was ten members left. Nine of them could not leave here alive, or I'd have an even bigger problem on my hands. I fired off another round of shots, but before I could see how many coven members went down, a man stepped in front of me.

No . . . not a man. A demon.

His shadow eclipsed me entirely.

My breath stuttered.

"That was unwise," the demon said.

"Oh?" I replied, considering my options.

He stared at me with an intensity hotter than the sun. The black flames in his eyes seemed to be reaching for me, wanting to set me on fire. I stumbled back, and he clasped both hands around my wrists.

"You called me into this world. You asked to bargain. Then you dare attempt to kill me—to run from me." The rage in his voice called to something within me. He leaned forward, his nose skimming my blood-splattered jaw. The demon followed the trail to the hollow of my ear and down my throat. "You won't be going anywhere."

Faster.

Faster.

Faster.

My heart beat. I pulled, trying to break his grip, but it was like moving a mountain. He didn't budge an inch.

Panic blossomed in my chest. It was the spark, my wild, erratic emotions the fuel.

And then it happened.

My heart stopped.

I blinked. Red tinted my vision. Rage consumed me. I bared my teeth at the demon, who jerked back to see my face. He cocked his head, watching me curiously. Keenly.

I pushed at him again, and this time he budged.

Surprise flared in his eyes.

My foot slammed into his shin at the same

moment my hands dropped. I flung my head forward, into his nose. I followed it up using all my strength and momentum to spin on my heel and aim an elbow-shot at his jaw.

Another crack echoed through the cathedral.

I turned to run and one of his hands tightened around my wrist once more.

The rage hammering through me burned bright. Blinding. I clenched my fist, and white flames erupted down my arm, fueled by the intensity of my hatred.

I opened my palm and unleashed every bit of fire I had in me.

The blazing inferno slammed into his chest, sending him flying.

He landed in the center aisle between the pews. Marble cracked under the impact.

I didn't stick around at that point. One quick sweep told me the members of the Antares Coven were long gone.

Which meant not only did I lose any bargaining power with the demon by refusing him, but now I'd also lost Claude Lewis.

The white fire died down, and with it, the unholy rage lifted. I was still angry, but not like before. Red still tinted my vision, and I knew it would be longer before the other side effects passed.

Unfortunately, now I had an even bigger problem. Several of them, really.

Gritting my teeth, I bolted down the hall and out the back door. The metal panel banged against the brick siding, the sound ricocheting down the alley. I stepped outside and slammed the door shut behind me, taking off the way I'd come.

As I rounded the corner, two of the cloaked members stood there.

I lifted my gun, and a sharp masculine command had the metal barrel crumpling inward. I cast it aside. Speaking low under her breath, the witch started to chant softly. The warlock next to her quickly joined in.

My muscles locked. My feet became leaden. I froze on the spot, unable to move.

Wind blew and lifted the edge of the taller one's hood, showing the face of a young man, only a few years younger than me, by the looks of it. He took a couple of steps toward me. It wasn't a very smart move, even if I were temporarily paralyzed, but they'd run from the cathedral before they saw what went down in there. They didn't know the half of what I was.

"Grab her," the girl hissed, stopping her chanting. The spell held, but only just. I could feel it start to weaken immediately.

"Do you see her eyes?" the warlock asked, stopping his own incantation. "They're red—"

"I don't give a damn what her eyes look like, Nathan. Grab her before—"

I bared my teeth in a malicious smile, and the warlock in front of me paled. His already milk-colored skin turning the color of bone.

"You're a—" he started to say. I lunged forward and sunk my fangs into his neck. Blood touched my lips, and a ravenous hunger threatened to consume me. I bit down hard, and then snapped back, spitting. A chunk of his flesh hit the cold pavement.

The warlock lifted a hand to his throat. Shock running through him.

He collapsed to his knees and then toppled sideways, bleeding out.

I raised my eyes to the girl before me.

In her fear, she didn't even try to stop me.

It was the greatest mistake she could have made.

I rushed her, and she lifted her hands in surrender.

"Please don't eat me," she cried.

I narrowed my eyes, seeing my own reflection in her dilated pupils.

Blood covered my lips and ran down my chin, splattering my coat.

I looked like a monster.

But I suppose I was one.

Just like them.

I backhanded her hard enough that her body half whipped around before her head hit the alley wall. She toppled to the cracked pavement, unconscious.

I sighed. To carry her, or to drag? Hard question. I was still mulling over the answer when an inhuman roar shook the very ground I stood on. Not wasting time, I bent my knees, slipped one arm around her back and the other beneath her knees. Hoping like hell she didn't wake up, I took off down the alley, as fast as my legs would carry me.

Heads turned as I bolted down the main road. My energy was flagging, and fast. I didn't usually tap into my other side. While powerful, it was draining.

Not to mention unnatural, my brain inserted. All magic had its price, and the price of using mine took its toll on my body.

Slowly, the red faded from my vision, and with it, the strength and speed I'd possessed.

This mission had been a complete and utter shit show.

I'd unleashed a demon on earth for nothing.

I'd let those bastards live for nothing.

I took a ragged breath, the girl in my arms still unconscious.

"Not for nothing," I muttered. I lifted my head and surveyed my surroundings. I was a block away from an L station. New Chicago kept the old metro system, but what was once public transport powered by electricity was now just another part of my past controlled by magic. While I usually avoided it like the plague, my options were limited if I wanted to get out before the demon found me. I may already be too late.

Screams sounded in the night. They were coming from the direction I'd just escaped.

I glanced over my shoulder just as the demon stepped beneath a streetlight.

I swallowed hard, and my feet took off. The soles of my boots thudded against the cobblestone as I veered right and headed for the station.

In the old days, you presented a card to enter and your money was subtracted. These days, the method of payment was infinitely more and less, depending on who you were.

At the sliding gates, instead of a reader for a card, a single needle jutted out.

My eyes flicked between it and the train approaching.

A shrill whistle blew, and people crowded the doors. I took one look behind me.

The demon was a mere twenty yards away.

His silver gaze burned into me.

Shifting my hold, I clumsily held the witch's body with one arm as I lifted her hand and stabbed the fatty part of her palm down on the needle. It was probably a bit overkill, given that the payment required was only a single drop of blood, but I didn't have it in me to feel bad.

The barrier flashed green, and I bolted to the

other side.

I sensed more than saw the demon run for me. I pumped my legs as the train let out a second shrill trill. My foot just touched the train floor as the doors started to close. I stepped inside and turned around.

On the other side of the plastic window the demon lifted his hand and blasted the entire machinery apart that controlled the entry and exit of the trains. He started for me, that black fire in his eyes threatening to set me aflame.

Then the wheels started moving.

A slow smile curled up my lips as we gained speed. He ran beside the train, keeping pace with my window until we hit the tunnel. Darkness took over. The metal contraption shook. Bodies were packed in. Men and women pushed up against walls. Children cried, and the homeless solicited acts of entertainment for scraps of food or coin—not that the latter did much good. Most places no longer took physical money because witches and warlocks were prone to scamming people. Still, solicitors took any and every-thing they could get because in this world, nothing was free.

The L smelled of desperation and depravity, but as the train shot out from a tunnel, and the cloudy sky opened up, I sighed in relief.

I'd come toe-to-toe with a demon, and I'd lived.

This time.

I sagged against the double doors, looking through the foggy plastic at the city below. My relief at getting away slowly faded as worry tinged it, seeping in like ink on paper.

A niggling feeling ate at me. As relieved as I was to be alive, this was far from over.

6

THE DEMON

My hands clenched into fists.

There was a pounding in my ears and everything aside from the retreating lights of the moving train faded in a cloudy haze.

She ran from me.

I unclenched my fists and took a few hard breaths, trying to settle into this new form. It was different from my previous one. More confined. Contained. It held all that I was beneath a sinewy package of muscle and bone. Once, I would have hated it.

However, thousands of years of searching for her made me ambivalent. I didn't particularly care which form I took, as long as it led to her.

She ran from me. The words repeated in my mind, but I did not feel pain like one might expect. A hint of anger was there, but more than anything it was a driving desire to hunt her. Find her.

I had to know who this female was, and why she ran.

The distant roar of another train approaching pulled my attention back to my surroundings. I looked over the disgusting train station. It was so unlike the world I'd come from.

To find her, first I needed to understand this plane. While my magic made it possible for me to communicate with all life-forms, it did not grant me instant knowledge. That I had to take.

The two warlocks I'd killed in the cathedral gave me enough to understand some things, but they didn't know who my mystery female was, or why she wanted their leader alive.

No matter. All I needed to do was retrace my steps and follow the trail.

I'd find the leader that created the door between realms, figure out why she wanted him, and then use him to track her down.

She could run all she wanted. She wouldn't be able to evade me forever. I'd waited too long for her. I followed her from my world and into this one. If I had to, I'd follow her into the next.

There was no escaping me.

7

I GROANED, climbing the last few steps. While she wasn't very big, the cloaked witch was heavy when it was pouring rain outside and the water weighed us both down. My clothes were mostly dry from my shoulders to the knee where my trench coat ended. From there down had been soaked to the bone in icy cold water.

I shivered and leaned against the doorway as I let the witch's body slide down my own. My arms were shaking from the exertion of carrying her so far. While I was strong, I wasn't Superwoman. Especially when the crash hit.

My fingers fumbled with the ties on my jacket as I worked to open it and dug out my key from one of the inner pockets. I touched the end of the bronze fob to the panel on the door. It beeped once, and the tiny light at the top of it changed from red to green.

I wrapped my hand around the handle and the door swung open on its own. Sighing once more, I bent down and hauled the witch up as carefully as I could manage. While I didn't have much left before the crash, I needed to get her tied up before she woke.

I took one last look up and down the stairs, checking my neighbors' apartments. All was quiet, and as far as I could tell, not a soul knew I'd brought an unconscious woman back.

"Good," I muttered under my breath as I stumbled inside. Using the toe of my boot, I nudged the door, and it swung shut behind me, closing with an audible click. There was a whirring sound before the lock went back into place.

My apartment was spacious, at least by most human standards. Two bedrooms, a working bathroom, kitchen, and living room. It was filled with mismatched but comfortable furniture. The floors were fake wood, but they looked nice, just a bit scuffed. In this age, my apartment was the cream of the crop for a human. Because of our lack of gifts, we scraped the bottom of the barrel. The unwanted leftovers. There weren't many people that were well-off unless they had magic. Then again, I wasn't completely human. Not that anyone but a demon I'd set loose in the city knew that. I pressed my lips together, kicking the chair leg from under the shoddy dining table. I dropped my guest in the seat, arranging her so that she wouldn't fall over while I went to grab rope and a dishrag from the kitchen.

She was just beginning to stir when I came back. I stuffed the rag between her parted lips and tied it tight behind her head. Her eyes were fluttering open when I pulled the knife from my coat and cut a length of rope. I grabbed both her arms and pulled them taut behind her before she gained full consciousness.

My nimble fingers wound the rope tight around her wrists and in between her fingers. The latter was unusual, until you considered that some witches could do magic without words. I had no idea if she fell in that group. It was safer to make sure she had no use of her hands or her mouth, though.

I was just tying off the knot when she pulled against them.

A scream of outrage left her, but it was muffled by the rag as she tried and failed to pull at my binding. I came around to kneel in front of her. Flashes of hot then cold ran through me. Dizziness was impending. The crash was upon me. I had minutes at most. Which meant I'd better not fuck this up.

She kicked out, and I took one to the mouth before I managed to catch both her legs.

Blood scented the air. A mild pain broke through the numbness setting in.

She'd split my lip.

I smiled, knowing it would scare her more than anger her further.

She shuddered. I lifted my knife.

"Kick me again and I will plant this in your thigh," I said in a low tone. Her eyebrows furrowed. Indecision warred in her expression as she debated how serious I was. "You saw me rip your coven member's throat out with my bare teeth. You wanna test it?"

Her face paled, the fight draining out of her muscles even as she glared at me.

I didn't have it in me to smile again as I tied her lower limbs to the wooden legs of the chair. My hands were visibly shaking when I finished. I reached up, gripping the edge of the nicked wooden table to drag myself to my feet. By the time I was standing, spots danced in my vision.

I started for my bedroom. If the witch made a fuss about me leaving her like that, I didn't hear it. The sound of my heart beating was a riot in my head. Blood pounded as the mother of all migraines hit me. I reached out, pressing my forehead against the door as I fumbled with the knob, trying to twist it.

Nothing beyond the gray cotton sheets in my bedroom registered. I pulled at my coat, letting it drop

55

to the floor at my feet. Next, I peeled off my long-sleeved shirt. I took another step forward, half collapsing on my bed. The black spots in my vision were growing. The pain consuming. I reached for the laces on my boots, pulling at them furiously. I yanked on the heel of either boot, tossing both shoes aside, then laid back on the knock-off memory foam mattress.

I'd wanted to strip my pants as well. The bottom half was wet, and the air was cold. It was December in New Chicago, and not a dry one. Past the jackhammer pounding in my brain, and the twitching of my muscles, I didn't have it in me to hold off the crash any longer.

My eyes fell closed, and darkness welcomed me.

HOT FLASHES PLAGUED ME, followed by bouts of freezing cold. I alternated between shivering and sweating as nightmares held me under. I dreamed of my past and present, of the mistakes I'd made. The things I'd done. The people that had died in the cross-fire along the way.

I dreamed of *him*.

The demon that hunted me.

Black fire danced in my dreams. Lighting everything I'd seen aflame until only the ashes remained.

When I finally opened my eyes, cold sweat coated my skin. My muscles felt sore, and my head still pounded.

The crash, as I'd called it, had run my body through the wringer.

I let out a shaky breath, my abdomen clenching as I hauled myself up in a sitting position. The door to my bedroom was wide open. Between here and there, my clothes littered the floor, like I'd had a one-night stand after too many drinks. Unfortunately, that was not the case.

If the clothes weren't proof enough, the grunt that came from my living room reminded me just how much I'd fucked up my last mission.

I glanced over at the battery-powered clock on my nightstand. It was past four in the afternoon.

I got to my feet and dragged my exhausted ass out of my room and toward the bathroom. Another grunt drew my attention as the witch I'd captured pulled at her bindings. For someone that had cowered right before I knocked her unconscious, she was being awfully brave.

I turned on my heel and lifted both eyebrows. Whatever I was going to say dried up on my tongue as I took one look at her. Light brown hair stuck up in odd angles, strands of it were plastered against her sweaty face. Her lips were chapped, and her cheeks splotched and ruddy. The brown eyes that stared back at me were bloodshot and angry.

She was sick.

The grunts weren't simply for my attention, but to clear her throat. Or at least attempting to.

I'd left her in her wet, sopping cloak for I don't know how long, and I was too cheap to pay for heat. While most supernatural creatures wouldn't fall ill to the elements, or anything else, witches and warlocks were the weakest on that front. Their bodies were mortal.

I let out a sigh. This was really the last thing I needed to deal with right now.

Not when I needed answers.

My eyes strayed to the second bedroom.

"I'm going to shower, and once I feel human again—I'll try to figure out a solution for your . . ." My words trailed. Her eyes narrowed. "Predicament."

Turning on my heel, I shut myself in the bathroom. Not wanting to look at my reflection, I flipped the shower on and stripped the rest of the way. I clambered in as soon as steam started to rise above the curtain. It wasn't until I was washing the conditioner out of my hair that I noticed the bruises around my wrists.

The memory of his hands wrapped around me, his skin pressing against my own. It made me shiver.

Hatred, I told myself. *Disgust.*

He was a demon. Not a man. Not truly.

I finished washing myself and flipped the water off. Shoving the curtain aside, I stepped out onto the plastic bathmat. With a faded pink towel, I dried my skin and wrung my long blonde hair out in the tub.

When I opened the bathroom door, cold air kissed my skin. I strode across my tiny living room and closed the door behind me when I entered my bedroom, letting the towel drop.

First thing, I rehung my trench coat and emptied it of weapons. Then I dressed in black jeans and another long-sleeved shirt. Using a utility belt, I strapped a gun on each hip.

I opened my bedroom door and regarded the witch coolly.

"Now, you and I are going to have a little chat. If you're good, I'll give you food and medicine—and maybe even let you use the bathroom. If you're not," I paused to lift one of my guns for her to see. "I have zero problem shooting you."

She continued to glare as I approached her. Kneeling in front of the chair, I lifted the gun and pointed it in her direction, before yanking the gag from her mouth.

She coughed twice, and I could see it in her expression that she was debating which was the worse evil. Being alive and questioned, or having me kill her.

"What do you want?" she asked.

I smiled, but it wasn't kind. "The same thing I always want from your kind. Answers."

She shifted in her chair, clearly uncomfortable, but compliant—at least for the moment.

"To?"

"Why did the Antares Coven want to summon a demon?" I asked, without missing a beat.

She laughed once, humorlessly. "Why does any coven try a summoning?" she asked rhetorically. "Power," she spat the word.

I narrowed my eyes. "You sound like you don't agree."

Her expression hardened before closing down entirely. Her eyelids fluttered, lowering so I couldn't read her expression as easily. "I'm not hearing a question."

"The Antares Coven summoned it for power. Why did you summon it?"

"I'm part of the Antares Coven," she answered simply. The problem was that I got the impression this was anything but simple.

I rocked back on my heels, letting my butt hit the floor, but still holding the gun extended. I rested my arm on my bent knee. "Why did you join the Antares Coven?"

She smiled, and it was bitter. "It was expected of me."

"Expected?" I repeated, sensing her vulnerability.

"I come from a strong line. A pure line," she said, her voice acidic, yet soft. "It was expected of me."

"Which family?" I asked.

"What?" she blinked, as if realizing what she'd said.

"Which family do you come from?" There were over a dozen families of witches and warlocks that came from old magic. They were pious fools, but not toward some unknown god. They held themselves and their blood to a standard above us all. They believed themselves the closest thing we had to gods on this earth. They were only loyal to their own power-hungry lust.

The witch laughed once more, shaking her head. "You won't get a ransom for me," she said. I had no intention of ransoming the girl, not that she knew that.

"Why is that?"

Her lips pressed together. "I'm the youngest of three daughters. The least gifted. I'm not married, and my coven attempted a summoning and failed. If you know half as much as you claim, you know that my family won't pay. Not for a failure."

Ah. I understood it easily then.

"You're a Le Fay."

She blinked slowly. "How'd you know that?"

"I make it my business to know things. It's not

easy surviving this world as a human. Knowledge is power."

"You're not human." She said it as a statement, but it implied a question. One corner of my mouth curled upward.

"No," I said softly. "I suppose I'm not."

"I thought you were a vampire," she started, hesitant. "But you're not. You're something else." Her eyes squinted. She was trying to figure me out. Turn the tables and glean any little bit of information I gave her.

"How do you know I'm not a vampire?"

"Your lip," she answered. I lifted my free hand to my face and remembered that before the crash, she'd headbutted me and split my lip. I chuckled under my breath.

"You're young to be in a coven already. Especially one as ambitious as Antares. Did you choose them? Or did your parents?" I asked her, redirecting the conversation. She let out a raspy breath that I'm pretty sure was her attempt at a sigh, were she not so congested.

"My parents," she said. "They knew the Antares were planning a summoning. If it succeeded, I could become one of the most powerful witches of the age. Redeem myself in their eyes. If it didn't . . ." she trailed off, lifting her eyes to meet mine.

"You died, and they didn't have a disappointment for a daughter anymore," I surmised.

Harsh, but true for witches and warlocks.

"What do you want from me?" she repeated.

"I already told you. Answers. Tell me what you know about Claude Lewis."

"Claude Lewis?" she asked, the name clearly not ringing a bell.

"The leader. The one trying to command the demon," I supplied.

"Kenneth du Lac," she spat. "He's a bastard."

I'd never heard of Kenneth du Lac, though I knew the last name. That explained a lot about how I'd never been able to find him, even after all these years. Claude Lewis was simply an alias. One that I'd believed back then and didn't realize I should have known better until now.

"How so?"

She narrowed her eyes again. "You can piece together that I'm a Le Fay, but you don't know of Kenneth du Lac?" She sounded disbelieving.

"I want to hear it from you," I said, though it grated me because she was right. I did know a great deal about a great many things. I hadn't seen this, though, just as I hadn't realized he'd be there last night.

"He doesn't give a damn about his coven. All he

cares about is power, and he'll manipulate anyone he can to get it."

I nodded along as she spoke. "According to you, that's all anyone from Antares cared about."

"He's . . ." she searched for an ending. "Different. Worse than the others. While power was all the coven cared for, there were still rules in place. Precautions to shield from the darker costs of magic. Lines we didn't cross. If Kenneth thought it would get him more power, he'd sacrifice anyone and everyone for it."

I had to work to keep a straight face and not reveal anything.

While he went by a different name, he was certainly the same man I had been looking for.

"Do you know where I could find him?" I asked her.

"Not a clue. He kept his life outside the coven a secret. He was paranoid that someone was after him. And us by extension," her voice slowed. She blinked once. I knew the moment she put those two pieces together. "It was *you*."

"I searched a long time for him, but I was under the impression he was dead—until I saw him last night."

"Two nights ago," she corrected.

"What?"

"It's been two days. You were unconscious the first one."

It was like an icy wave had hit me full on as I realized I'd been out for over thirty-six hours.

Shit. Shit. Shit.

This was not good.

If I'd been unconscious that long, it meant the demon was loose that long. The odds that my boss wasn't aware that not only had I'd failed to kill the coven, but that I'd intentionally let them summon a demon was exponentially low at this point. I wouldn't have time to play this off with Anders. There was likely already a price on my head.

I took a deep breath.

"You look like I feel," the witch commented. I narrowed my eyes at her.

"I'd be wary of insulting me while I have this pointed at you," I said. Her eyes slid to the gun, but some of the earlier fear had edged.

"You don't want to kill me," she said, sounding awfully sure of herself. "I won't go so far as to say you need me, but you wouldn't have brought me back if you just wanted to shoot me."

"I was hired to kill you, you know?"

Surprise flickered in her eyes and a hint of fear returned to her expression.

"Not me specifically," she said, like that made it better somehow.

"No, your coven. I was supposed to put all thirteen of you six feet under before you summoned the demon." I motioned with the end of my gun and the rise and fall of her chest sped up. The pulse in her neck quickened. Her body told me all I needed to know about what she was feeling, but her face did not. She kept it guarded behind sickness and distrust.

"So why didn't you?"

It was a simple question, really, with a simple answer.

"I was going to bargain for information from the demon and then kill you all, but I hadn't realized the man I knew as Claude would be there." I talked about her death as if it were the weather. For a moment, I wondered if that made me as bad as the monsters I hunted. Then I realized, of course I was as bad as them.

Much as I thought of myself as human, I wasn't.

We were one and the same.

"But you didn't." Her eyebrows drew together. "You tried to get the demon to kill us instead, so you could go after Kenneth."

I nodded. "I thought I could get the information I needed without having to rely on a creature that only *might* give me what I want. Demons are notoriously mercurial."

"You gave up the bird in your hand for the two in the bush," she said on a dry croak. "And now you have a demon hunting you, Kenneth du Lac is smoke in the wind, and my coven still lives. At least enough of it does. Whoever hired you had deep pockets and many eyes. They will know you failed by now."

"How do you figure that?" I asked, mildly impressed she'd been able to deduce as much in her current state.

"I heard what he asked for before you shot him. He wants you." She looked me over, seeming to think about that before continuing. "And you ran. The demon isn't going to just give up, you know?"

I tilted my head. "How much do you know about demons?"

A dry chuckle escaped her lips that quickly turned into a cough. After hacking for thirty-five seconds, she took a deep breath before saying, "Some. Not a lot. I get the impression you know more." Her eyes dropped to my throat where the long-sleeved shirt covered me.

"Probably," I murmured, picking at a loose thread on my jeans.

"My coven, what's left of it, will have assumed I'm on the run. If I'm not already excommunicated from my people, I will be by tomorrow."

I lifted an eyebrow. While the thought hadn't occurred to me yet, she wasn't wrong. Any that weren't dead would be labeled as either a traitor or a coward. What I couldn't figure out, was why she would bring my attention to that.

"What do you want?"

Another dry chuckle slid between her lips. "You're

straightforward. I like that," she said. "I want to work with you."

"Why?"

"A witch without a coven to protect her is a dead one. Same for wolves without a pack. Vampires without a clan. We all need someone in this new world order." She didn't look away. Where many of her kind would rather lop off a limb than admit their own shortcomings, she leaned into it. "Except for you. If you're strong enough to live and get away from both a demon and a coven—you're strong enough that I want to be on your side."

I blinked. "I work alone."

"And how much good did that do you?" she asked, descending into a fit of coughing.

"By your own admission, you're not a gifted witch. You wouldn't last on your own, whereas I managed to capture you, evade a demon, and take out some of the Antares Coven. You'll only hold me back," I replied.

She sniffed once. "Maybe. Maybe not. I can help you find Kenneth du Lac, though. Whatever you want from him, you risked everything to get it. I have to think that's worth something."

It was worth everything, but I didn't tell her that. In this world, knowledge was power, and I'd already said too much.

"I work alone," I repeated. Leaning forward, I

reached for the rag to stuff it back in her mouth. For the first time since we'd started talking, she struggled against her bonds.

"Wait! I can help—"

A knock at my door made me pause.

I sat back, looking between my hostage and the door.

"If you so much as try to curse me—"

"That's not a convincing strategy when I'm wanting you to work with me," she said. I pressed my lips together, slowly getting to my feet.

There was no way in hell that was happening, but instead of telling her that, I put a finger to my lips in the universal sign of silence. She nodded.

Quietly, I made my way toward the door, walking softly and using my knowledge of the apartment not to step on a creaky board.

Not once in the last ten years had I given my address out, and people didn't just come knocking on a door in this age. Not unless they wanted to end up full of lead.

Which meant it was one of three parties standing outside.

The sick churning in my gut had a feeling which, and I wasn't sure if it were better or worse than the others.

I peered through the peephole.

Anders stood on the other side.

Wedging myself between the door and the rest of my apartment, I pulled the gun from my left holster and cracked the door, angling the barrel of my firearm through the three-inch gap.

"Why are you here?" I asked him, not wasting time.

He stared at me, and I saw the answer in his eyes.

"You fucked up, Pip. You fucked up big."

8

"How'd you know where to find me?"

He gave me a scathing look, like I knew better than to ask that. "Can I come in?"

I raised the gun until it was chest level, then repeated myself. "How did you know where to find me?"

"Come on, Pip. You're not going to shoot—"

A flick of my wrist was all it took. The barrel of the gun swung downward. I pulled the trigger. The shot echoed through the empty corridor, but not a single one of my neighbors opened their doors to see what was up.

I would say they were smart, but the truth was less complimentary. They were self-serving. Surviving. You didn't get far in this world by sticking your nose where it didn't belong, and the people in this building knew when to butt out.

Anders staggered, taking a single step back. He reached behind him and gripped the railing. His face was pale, and lips pinched together.

Red formed a puddle around his left foot.

"How did you know where to find me?" I asked, and it was the last time I was going to. "Answer the question, or the next one goes in your brain, Anders."

"I had you followed," he said. Panted breaths punctuated his words with pain.

"When?"

"Last year," he answered. His knuckles had gone white and his knees trembled.

"Why?"

His eyes rose from the gun he was still staring at to look me in the face. "You had made a name for yourself."

"That doesn't answer the question." I raised the gun once more, this time angling it at his shoulder.

"You have the highest kill count out of any of our hunters. The highest success rate of capture. The boss took notice. He got curious."

"He decided I was dangerous enough that you wanted some reassurances if I ever left," I surmised.

He gave me a tight nod. "I was sent to deliver a message."

I lifted an eyebrow. "Do tell."

Anders' breath grew harder, more erratic. He wasn't so used to the pain.

"Three days," he said through gritted teeth.

"Three days?" I repeated softly.

"To clean up the mess you made."

I stared at him unblinking. "The mess I made?"

"You didn't come back. Rumors came to our door instead of you. The boss tracked down one of the coven members himself. They told him what happened, Pip. He knows that you *chose* to let it happen when you could have stopped it. He wants the coven dealt with, and the demon put down."

"Demons aren't easy to kill," I replied, my voice terse.

His posture was stiff, more rigid than I'd ever seen it, and I wasn't sure if that was because of the situation, or the bullet I'd just put through his foot. "You should have thought of that before you let them summon it."

"What happens after three days?" My voice had dropped, the tone soft, but not kind.

"He puts a price on your head," Anders replied. I didn't let my face reveal the stuttering beat that ran through my chest.

"How much?"

His eyes narrowed. "You did not just ask me—"

"Do you really want to finish that sentence while you're still bleeding out on my doorstep?" My eyes flicked down to the puddle of blood that had grown considerably in the time we were standing here. He had to be feeling lightheaded by now.

"One million," he croaked. The pain was getting to him.

I let out a low whistle. "That's twice as much as he offered for the coven."

"You let them summon it. You know how he takes to betrayal."

Betrayal. Like I owed him allegiance of any sort. My boss was a job, a complicated one, a demanding one, but a job, nonetheless. Any other person would have understood this wasn't personal. It wasn't about allegiance or loyalty or trust.

But it was my boss we were talking about. He was prickly by nature.

"Three days to deal with the coven and the demon. I still get paid at the end?"

A harsh laugh echoed through the stairwell. "Only you would ask about a paycheck after what you've done." I lifted the gun once more, this time pressing it into his forehead, between the eyes. He sighed. "You're a cold woman, you know that?"

"So you've told me," I replied.

"I don't know if he'll pay you. I don't know if he'll just execute you on the spot. You really pissed him off with this one, Piper."

Honesty it was, then. I appreciated it, even though I'd never tell him that.

I lowered the gun to my side, and he let out a breath.

"Three days?" I said, not looking at him.

"Three days," he repeated with a nod. I stepped back and moved to close the door. "Be careful, Pip."

I paused, one corner of my mouth twisting ruefully. "Shouldn't I be saying that to you?"

"You did just shoot me," he said, dragging his foot sideways as he tried to change his hold on the rail.

"And I will again if you don't get out of here. I have three days before every bounty hunter in this city comes after me. See you soon, Anders."

I closed the door before he had time to reply, and then leaned forward, putting my forehead against it. *Fuck.*

On one hand, I was lucky he didn't just put out an immediate hit, but all that really meant is they didn't have someone as equipped as I was to clean up this job. And unlike the hit on me, this isn't something they'd want the public to know about. Demons coming to earth caused panic. Rightfully so.

The real reason my boss didn't want a demon in New Chicago had less to do with the people, and more to do with his own addiction to power.

"Did you just shoot someone in the stairwell?" the

witch asked. She must have taken the door closing as a sign it was all safe to talk again.

"Yup."

"But you didn't kill them?" she squinted her eyes, trying to understand.

"How do you know that?"

"You closed the door. I can't imagine you would have left a dead body on your own doorstep. Great way to lure all bloodsuckers out, and that's the last thing you need right now."

I gave her an appraising look. She wasn't stupid.

"It was a warning."

"The person at the door, or you shooting them?"

"Both," I answered. "Still want to work with me?"

She blinked. Then a rasped chuckle slid between her lips. "Yes."

"The man at the door—" I nodded my head in the direction of it. "I worked with him for years. He's as close to a friend as I've had, and I just put a bullet in him. Are you sure?"

"I stand by what I said before. I'm a dead woman by myself. I could help you, though."

Her face was an open book. Easy to read. It was an odd thing for a witch. They were almost as cold as the fae.

"I don't like witches," I told her.

"Neither do I," she responded immediately.

"I don't like magic. I don't like supernaturals. I'm

used to working alone because I don't play nice with others. I'm an asshole—and I'm telling you all this because if you give me any reason at all to think you betrayed me—putting a bullet in you will be the least that I will do."

"What made you change your mind?" she asked, instead of answering.

"I have three days. I'm good. Really good. But I can't find and kill the remaining members of the Antares Coven in three days on my own. Let alone a demon."

I let the words sink in. She lifted both eyebrows and let out a slow exhale.

"They expect you to kill the demon?"

I nodded. "Does that scare you?"

"Yes," she answered instantly. "But it doesn't change my answer. I've been a Le Fay for twenty-two years. I've seen a lot in that time. Not once have I seen someone take on a full coven like you did. Killing a demon might be impossible, but I'm willing to gamble my life on it if you're who I'm working with."

I strode around the chair and came up behind her. Pulling the knife from the table beside me. I moved slowly, letting her see and contemplate her response.

When I pressed the blade to her neck, she swallowed hard, but she didn't try to curse me.

I dropped the blade to her wrists and cut the bindings restraining her.

Air hissed between her teeth as she slowly moved her hands around in front of her and began rubbing at them.

"One chance. That's all you get with me." I stepped around to the front of her chair and knelt down, cutting the rope holding each of her legs to the wooden pegs.

"I won't waste it," she vowed. Raising her blood-shot eyes to meet my own.

"We'll see." I shrugged, stepping back.

Whoever this witch was, her life meant little to me. It was only because of my own shit situation and her intriguing honesty that I was even entertaining this.

"What happens at the end of the three days if we fail?" she asked.

My expression didn't change as I said, "Every bounty hunter in the city will be after me, and if you've lived that long—you too."

She swallowed hard and nodded. "I guess we should get to work, then."

A smile threatened to break through because part of me was starting to like her. Despite her heritage. Despite our differences. If we were both human, we would have made good friends.

But neither of us were.

"There are towels in the bathroom. Get yourself cleaned up. I'll find you clean clothes and medicine."

I was already moving toward my bedroom once

more when the witch said, "I'm Nathalie, but my friends call me Nat. What's your name?"

I didn't pause in my stride. My hand reached for the bedroom doorknob and twisted it open. "Piper," I said. "Piper Fallon."

9

Twenty minutes later, she stood in my living room, dripping water from her shoulder-length brown hair. A ratty yellow towel was tucked under both her arms, and while her eyes looked clearer, her nose was still red.

I held out a stack of clothes. "You're shorter than me, but these should be a close fit."

She took them, muttering her thanks, and returned to the bathroom. What I didn't tell her was that the clothes weren't mine. I'd gone into the second bedroom of my apartment while she was showering and rummaged through the drawers until I'd found something that looked both warm enough and the right size.

Several minutes later she stepped back out. A long olive-green shirt hugged tightly to the curve of her breasts but fit loose in the waist. The dark skinny jeans from an era long gone were snug, but not enough to make me go look for a different pair. Underneath the sickness, she was a pretty girl, not that she seemed to notice. I didn't comment as I stepped around the counter that separated the living room from the kitchen. I gathered all the fruit on the counter and pulled out a cutting board. Nowadays, anything fresh was hard to come by. When I did get it, it was so expensive I could only afford it after it was past its prime, and the rich people no longer wanted it.

"What type of magic do you have?" I asked, cutting the inedible pieces away from the fruit. Nathalie came around the edge of the counter and crossed her arms over her chest, then leaned her hip against it.

There were three types of magic that witches and warlocks possessed.

White. Black. Gray.

None of them were better or worse than others, contrary to what some white magic users may have claimed. They didn't decide your power level, it merely guided in the realm of what you were good at.

White magic excelled in healing, potions, and most nature magic. In short, they specialized at harmony. Their magic naturally gravitated toward it. They worked well with others. Their magic played 'nice'.

Black did not. It was explosive. Aggressive. True black magic witches were rarer than white. They were inclined to attempt summonings and necromancy because their magic was more of a parasite than anything. It sought control.

Gray was somewhere in the middle.

In truth, it didn't matter what she was, but if I was going to be working with her, I needed to have some concept of what she was capable of, beyond the information she could provide about the Antares Coven.

"Gray," she answered. "But it's weak."

"Define weak." I tossed the fruit in a blender and added a splash of water. The grinding took all of thirty seconds. She waited patiently, only speaking once I turned it off.

"Le Fay is largely a black magic line. One of the few still around. Because I'm gray, that was viewed as flexible. My family thought I had the potential to be good at both, if not great—and that was acceptable." As she spoke, I pulled two plastic cups out and topped them both with the fruit smoothie. I slid one across the counter and took a rather large gulp of the other. "At least until I proved abysmal at all of it. I can't draw on nature. I'm a terrible healer. When I partook in a summoning to raise an aunt that died in the Magic Wars, I managed to raise her body and banish her spirit . . ." She shook her head at the memory.

"My magic doesn't play nicely with others, but spells still go awry when I work alone."

I took another long swallow from my smoothie and then lifted my eyes to her.

"You managed to bind me in the alley," I pointed out.

She sniffed. "That was mostly Nathan, he was my mentor in the Antares Coven. My parents had me paired with him because he was good with fighting incantations, and they hoped he'd grow to like me."

"Hoping to pawn you off for marriage?"

"Yup."

"He's probably dead, you know," I said, then took another long drink of liquid fruit. "And if he's not, I have to hunt him down. You can't stop me."

"I won't," she said solemnly. "I know you might find this hard to believe, but I don't care if they die. Maybe that makes me a traitor. Maybe I deserve to be excommunicated over it . . ." She ran her long nails over the plastic countertop. "But it's a dog-eat-dog world, you know? Everyone for themselves. As long as you have my back, I don't really give a damn what happens to the rest of Antares. The world's probably better off without them, anyway."

I dipped my head in acknowledgement.

"So, if you suck at all magic, what are you good at?"

"Remembering things. I have an eidetic memory,

and thanks to my family's interesting version of an education, I do know most spells, curses, hexes, potions—you name it."

"So, knowledge, in essence?" I asked. No judgement in my voice, though she clearly expected it.

"Yes . . ." Her voice trailed. "I know it's probably not what you were hoping for."

"Yes and no," I replied, turning away to rummage through my cabinets for food. "You having some sort of magic could be useful. More than dead weight. That said, I don't trust magic, or magic users. You start flinging around curses like a dick in a locker room and I'm bound to get a little twitchy."

"I may not be kickass in a fight, but I am crafty. I know how to hold my own around witches and warlocks," she said, slightly defensive.

"That's good, because if you expect me to save you from everything, you won't last long." When all I could find was stale crackers and moldy bread, I let out a sigh. Giving up on my search for food, I pulled one of my kitchen drawers open and rummaged through it.

I popped two pills from a plastic package and held my hand out.

To her credit, she didn't question me after her show of trust. She simply took the two pills and swallowed them down, along with the rest of her smoothie.

"Got any food?" she asked, her stomach letting out a loud gurgle in protest.

"Unfortunately, no. We're going to need to go out for that. The medicine should help dry you up, though," I said as she sniffled.

"Thank you for that."

My only response was to retreat into my bedroom and close the door behind me. I strapped on several more weapons and donned a baggy windbreaker to deal with the wind and rain. Stuffing my feet in my now dry boots and grabbing an extra jacket, I stepped back into the living room.

Nathalie was wearing her own pair of leather boots. At the sight of the jacket in my hand, her face brightened.

I handed it over to her silently and then motioned for her to walk ahead of me.

She went for the door and paused, looking at me for approval.

I cursed under my breath. "This isn't going to work if you have to ask me permission for every fucking thing you do."

Her mouth opened, then closed, as she grasped the handle and stepped into the hall.

Her eyes automatically went to the pool of blood Anders had left on my doorstep.

"Is that—"

"Yes," I replied, closing the door behind me. I

heard the audible whir as the latch clicked and the locking mechanism on my door activated once more.

"Should we clean it up—"

"Leave it," I said, putting a hand on her shoulder and pushing toward the stairs. "It reminds my neighbors to mind their own damn business in case any of them ever thinks about getting nosy."

She seemed to consider that as we started down the stairs. Our steps echoed all the way to the ground floor.

"You're a strange woman, Piper."

One corner of my mouth curled up in a cold grin as we stepped out into the alleyway.

"You don't even know the half of it."

THE DINER SMELLED like a heart attack and bad life choices. I sat across from Nathalie in the dingy booth. Grime lined the edge of the table from where they'd been too lazy to use a little elbow grease over the years. The floor was checkered, and the barstools were rusted.

Our waitress walked up and dropped our food off without two words. Her too tight shirt tugging at the second button where her breasts pulled at it. She wore leggings and an apron that served little more than to further cinch her waist. Judging by the other clientele

the cashier stand and did the same. The tips flashed from red to green, signaling the transfer went through.

"Pleasure, sweetness," she said, adding a little zing now that she knew I wasn't a complete asswipe.

"No need to lay it on for me. Save the *sweetness* for your clients that like it." I approached the table once more and was pleased to find her pancakes were nearly gone. "Ready?"

Nathalie took a long swig of her coffee, emptying the mug. It clapped down on the plastic table, and she moved to stand.

The door jingled as another party stepped in.

I lifted my head and one look told me there was going to be trouble. Thinking quick, I spun around. My hand locked on Nathalie's forearm as I debated going out the back.

Apparently, luck was not in my cards this evening.

"Piper? That you?" a southern drawl called out. I froze, cursing under my breath.

"Flint." My tone said it all. Unlike his that implied familiarity, mine was cold. Closed off. In other words, professional.

"I haven't seen you around, darlin'." His eyes roamed my form, and if he was disappointed, he didn't look it. "Where've you been?"

"Oh, you know. Here and there," I muttered, running my nails alongside the shitty table surface.

The sound of his boots as he came toward me made the rest of the diner fade. I needed to get out of here. Now wasn't the time for a trip down memory lane.

"You always did love the chase," Flint said, coming to stand before me. His pale blue eyes and light blonde hair were too clean, too polished for the diner.

I scoffed under my breath. "I've been busy. You know how it is."

Cold fingers touched my cheek, skimming down to my chin. I slapped his hand away, and my heart rate started to pick up.

Fuck no. This was not happening here.

A chuckle slid from his lips. "I've missed you, Pip."

I nudged Nathalie, telling her to start walking. "Afraid I can't say the same, Flint."

I moved to step around him and those cold fingers wrapped around my shoulder. "I heard there was an incident the other night. Your boss ain't so happy."

"Fuck off, Flint. It's none of your business."

The hand on my shoulder tightened. My heart rate picked up once more.

There was a fine line where one went from adrenaline junky to what I was. The faster my heart beat, the closer it was to stopping, and that couldn't happen.

If not for the fact that I'd kept my secret for ten

years, then because I couldn't afford for that sort of incident in a diner full of supes and humans alike. While I had no problems with killing, mass murdering innocents wasn't my style.

"You're in trouble, Pip. I can help."

Yeah right. More like he wanted a chance to fuck me again. Maybe more.

"You can help by keeping your nose, and your department, out of it. I left human patrol years ago, and I have no intention of going back. Now remove your hand from my shoulder."

I stared straight in his eyes and let him see I wasn't fucking around.

The fingers clamped around my shoulder slid away.

"I'm not giving up just yet," he said softly.

I didn't dignify that with a response as I followed Nathalie out of the diner, moving past several men I'd once worked with without so much of a hello.

We were a block away when Nathalie decided it was safe to pry.

"So," she drawled. "Who was that?"

"Old friend."

"By your own admission, you don't have friends."

I snorted. "Old fuck buddy," I corrected.

"He share that definition of you?" she replied.

"Doesn't matter. He's not our problem."

"That was Flint Daniels. He's head of human

patrol. Been working there for a decade. He rose faster in the ranks than any other member has managed to."

I glanced at her out of the side of my eye. "You wanna tell me how you know that?"

She tapped her head with her index finger. "I'm a witch with an eidetic memory. More often than not, human patrol traps supes because said supes don't know who they're dealing with. They get ambushed thinking they're taking home some drunk human, and it turns out to be a hunter. Harder to be trapped by one if you know who they are." She breathed a little harder as the wind blew, whipping the still damp strands of her hair around. "I suppose I should say rose faster than all with the exception of one."

"So, you do know who I am."

She shrugged once. "You were the best hunter they had, but you didn't like to play by the rules. Got your hands dirty too much. Had a knack for hunting witches and warlocks specifically . . ." Her voice trailed. "I assume that has to do with whatever Kenneth did to piss you off."

"Well, aren't you a smart witch?" I said sarcastically.

"You disappeared off record a few years ago, but you weren't reported dead. Given the talk about your boss, I take that to mean you just went to work for someone who didn't mind you playing a little dirty."

"Something like that," I muttered. I wasn't planning to tell her the actual reason I went after those witches and warlocks had very little to do with hunting Kenneth, and more to do with the reason I needed Kenneth at all.

"How do we find Greta?" I asked, noting that we'd walked several blocks already into a part of the city I was familiar with, but not intimately so. It was a supernatural sector. While humans could come in and out, it was ninety percent supes, if not more. Smart humans knew to avoid this place. Only those truly desperate set foot in this area.

"We don't," Nathalie said. "She's not hiding."

All at once she came to a stop. I looked up at the building.

Sin.

The letters shone in bright, glowing purple. It was one of the biggest supe clubs, and one of the shadiest places in New Chicago.

"Greta is a little too vain for her own good. Combine that with her power-hungry nature, she comes here looking for a man with enough juice so that it's worth her time."

Aka, she harvested magic. Something that was a crime, not that it was ever enforced unless you did it to the wrong person.

"She'd come here, even after the summoning?" I asked.

"She'd come here *because* of the summoning. She's a mid-level black witch. She's going to need all the power she can get to keep herself alive when it's every man for themselves."

I couldn't argue with that. Nathalie started for the door, and I paused her.

"If this is a trap, I don't think I have to tell you how sorry—"

"Piper, the fact that I'm aligning with you should say all there is to know about my loyalties. I don't know you. I just know of you, and I've seen what you can do. Believe me when I say, I have no intention of screwing you over. You're my best chance of staying alive."

I searched her expression, and while none of the telltale signs of a liar were there, it was still hard to trust her. I motioned with my hand for her to go first, and Nathalie smiled.

I really, really hoped I wasn't going to regret this.

I stared at the hybrid's back as he escorted us back to the staircase and started climbing.

"She must have really pissed him off."

We got to the top of the stairs where a balcony wrapped around the entire club, overlooking the festivities below. Beyond that, a much nicer lounge took up most of the space. The lights were so low I could only make out bodies, but not who they were or what they were doing.

"She tortured him growing up, and their parents did nothing," Nathalie muttered back.

Ouch. Witches and warlocks really were some of the worst of the lot as far as supernaturals went. I had a feeling, based on his features, the kid was a by-product of adultery, likely the mother.

"I don't want your pity," Barry said, without looking at me. That fae hearing of his must come in handy.

"You don't have it," I replied.

He regarded me coolly before nodding once. "I don't particularly care what you do about my sister as long as she doesn't know I helped you."

"You won't have to worry about that when I'm done."

His yellow eyes blinked, then he nodded.

"Follow this around the left side to the last door on the right. She'll be in there."

With that, Barry turned and kissed Nathalie on the check.

"Thanks, Barry," she whispered softly.

"Be safe, Nat." He glanced sideways at me, and Nathalie gave him a tight smile.

I started down the carpeted walkway that hugged the glass railing overlooking the club.

"Don't take it personal—" Nathalie started, walking fast to keep up with my longer gait. I didn't slow down.

"I don't," I replied. "He'd be an idiot to trust me."

She snorted. "You know for someone that needs help, you sure like reminding me that you could turn on me."

"Need is a bit of a stretch here," I said as we approached the door.

"You're not keeping me around for my charming personality or badass magic," she deadpanned.

I almost grinned at that, but we were at the door.

I pulled a pistol from my holster. One that had a silencer on it. Thankfully, this being a supe club, there were no cameras to speak of, and the darkness provided me with a natural cloak. And unless anyone here was looking too closely—they'd never know anyone entered or left the room.

Just the way I liked it.

"So how do we do this—" Nathalie started. I grabbed the handle and flung the door open. The heavy scent of magic pulled at me, trying to calm the violence in my blood, but there was something else in the air as well. A faint smoke drifted over me, filling me with warmth. My core tightened. I grit my teeth.

Motherfucking witches.

God, I hated magic.

I took a step forward, and Nathalie muttered, "Alright, guess we're doing it this way."

Ignoring her, I followed the scent of smoke around the corner. It opened up into a larger bedroom. A king-sized bed took up most of the space.

In it, the witch I presumed to be Greta McArthur wore lingerie and was busy being pleasured by three different men.

None of them had yet to notice me, despite the intrusion. The sounds of the club filtered through, but they were faint. Someone without my greater hearing likely wouldn't hear them at all. Which brought up the question of how they'd yet to notice when the door opened.

I had a feeling the decorative gravity bong filling the room with a moderate aphrodisiac had a lot to do with it.

"I'm assuming you can't bind them," I said under my breath.

"Uh, I wouldn't rely on it if I were you."

I sighed.

This job was going to get fucking messy and fast. I

didn't believe in any gods, but I might need to start after I was done.

Lifting the pistol, I fired off two quick shots.

The man sitting behind her whose chest she braced against went limp as his head exploded in an impersonation of a Jackson Pollock painting. She didn't even have time to react before the one eating her out also lost his head. The back part of his skull decorated her naked abdomen, and his body went limp.

"Holy shit," Nathalie murmured in quiet awe—or fear—frankly, I wasn't sure which.

The third man who was sucking her breast turned as blood splattered his cheek.

I fired a third shot, right between the eyes, and he dropped dead.

"Hello, Greta."

She opened and closed her mouth. I had to give it to her, I was surprised she didn't scream. More battle-hardened criminals than her had buckled under the initial shock of meeting me. My brand of acquiring information was far less appealing than Nathalie's.

Her throat bobbed. I couldn't make out her eye color in the low light, as her dilated pupils expanded.

Then at once, she recovered from her shock. She lunged to the side, starting a quick curse under her breath. I popped a shot that landed in her right hip

thickened. It was nearly tangible in the way it wrapped around me. My heart rate was nearing its climax.

I was dangerously close to coming undone.

And not in the good way.

"I couldn't find her. Now I know why. She was in the circle that called me, and yet here she is now with you . . ." His voice trailed off, as dark and deep as it was horribly lovely.

I should have shot myself right there, but I didn't.

His footsteps were silent as he came to stand before me.

To my credit, I didn't gasp in surprise, though I was utterly shocked to see him in a suit of all things. His dark hair was pulled back. His brands hidden beneath the tight fabric.

Silver eyes watched me. The world could have burned, but I had a feeling he wouldn't look away.

"You went after them," I said. "The coven. Why?"

The demon stepped forward and lifted a hand, brushing a strand of my honey-colored hair from my face. Black fire shone in his eyes. The same as before.

"You wanted one alive."

"What did that have to do with anything?" I asked.

"I needed to know why."

Faster.

Faster.

Faster.

My chest was squeezing painfully tight trying to contain my rapidly beating heart. His eyes dropped, and I had a feeling it had nothing to do with my tits.

The demon cocked his head.

"Do you?"

"Do I what?" he asked softly.

"Know why?"

He dragged his gaze back up my body, and it could have been his hands touching me for the way my skin set aflame. I almost worried that very real flames had broken out for a moment, but not quite. Not yet.

My heart still hadn't stopped.

"I do."

Those two words, they were my undoing.

I took a step back, and he took one forward.

My ribs ached as the beating organ in my chest reached a fever pitch.

I lifted my pistol to shoot and unload my entire magazine in his chest, but a hand closed around the barrel, crushing it instantly. My grip faltered, and he used the chance to fling the useless weapon aside.

I took another step back. He took another forward.

My back touched the wall.

Cornered. He had me cornered.

"Why do you want me?" I demanded.

A cruel grin twisted his lips. "Does it matter?" he asked, repeating himself from the first time we'd met.

"Yes."

"Liar," he growled. "You'd fear me no matter what I tell you. You hate me for what I am."

He reached for me with the same hand that easily crumpled a metal gun like paper. Fingers wrapped around my throat. Warm. Calloused. Immensely powerful. Magic invaded my pores with every touch.

"Does that matter?" I asked, repeating his own words back to him. "That I hate you for what you are?"

There was amusement in his gaze as he uttered, "Yes."

His face loomed closer. He leaned into me, and something feather soft skimmed my jaw. He stiffened.

Another growl left him, though for the life of me, I had no idea what I'd done.

"Who touched you?" he asked, his voice hardly human. I suppose that was to be expected, in a way, given he wasn't—but he sure did sound it at times.

"I don't know what you're talking about." I swallowed thickly.

"Liar," he said again, this time with heat. "I can smell *him* on you."

Him? Who the—

Realization hit me.

Before we'd come here, I'd been in the diner.

Flint had touched me.

"Who?" he asked again. A single word uttered softly had never sounded so deliciously damning.

"Does it matter?" I asked again. This question defined a lot. It answered a lot.

It confirmed a lot.

"Yes," the demon hissed. I closed my eyes.

Fuck.

There was no playing this off. He was definitely interested.

"Stop touching me," I snapped. It probably wasn't the wisest thing to say to a demon, mind you, but it was the best I had when my heartbeat was currently going a hundred miles an hour.

"No," he said. This time, the softness in his voice had something else there. Warmth. For the life of me, I couldn't understand why.

I growled in frustration, but that only seemed to encourage him. His lips barely touched me, but their shadow scalded what little skin they brushed against. Ecstasy ignited within me.

"You hate me. You hate my kind. But your body likes my touch," he whispered. "It loves it." He placed a hand on my hip, but was blocked from my skin by the holster at my side. "You are not like the humans. Weak of mind. Of will. Any other being, you would not feel this. Why do you think that is?"

He leaned back to see what was in his way, and I made a decision.

My heartbeat stopped.

Red tinted my vision as rage flooded. I slammed my foot down on his own, but the demon moved faster this time. He seemed to predict what was going to happen, because the moment my heart ceased to pound, he paused, his entire attention shifting.

Strong arms wrapped around me even as I tried to unleash myself on him.

"I knew you were in there," he murmured.

It was hard to land blows when he crushed me to his chest without actually crushing me. I reared back to slam my forehead into his nose. A crunch sounded. His grip didn't loosen in the slightest.

Power thickened as my magic rose with my rage. White fire consumed both my arms.

A pained hiss slid between his lips, but he held strong, or at least tried to.

My wild movements were harder to contain when I was on fire.

Two blows at his chest from my flaming fists sent him stumbling back.

The suit he was wearing now hung in tatters as it went up in a blaze. The white flames eating at it.

"I know who you are, Piper Fallon. I know *what* you are. I know why you hunted Kenneth du Lac, and I'd be willing to bet it's also why you called me from beyond," he said, stalking forward once more. "But you underestimated who you called. Who *I* am. You opened a door, and I smelled you, I felt your magic, I heard the beat of your heart—and it called to me like nothing in all this universe has. I am here because you *brought* me here, and no matter where you run—I will find you again."

I swallowed hard. The fire in me still burned. In this state, I was more susceptible to magic in the air than ever before. My baser survival instincts warped. I was burning, my emotions unraveling more with each passing moment as the aphrodisiac slipped into my skin and filled me with an awful fuzziness.

"Why?" I asked in an angry growl. The fangs that descended from my gums dripped with my blood and made my words convoluted.

"Because you're mine," the demon answered, as if it were so simple.

"I belong to no one," I answered. He smiled again, and while it was cruel, it was also pitying.

"You think that now," he said, looking up and down my form. "But I'll convince you. There is no other in this entire universe for you, woman."

I knew what he was saying, though he didn't use the word.

He must have seen it in my eyes because that pitying edge disappeared behind cruel amusement.

"Yes," he said softly. "You know what I speak of."

"I'm human. It's not possible."

"Maybe you were once." He scanned the white flames before staring in my eyes. "But you aren't human anymore. You're as bound by the laws of magic as any of us." The remaining pieces of his shirt fell away, revealing smooth, branded skin.

"You're lying," I snapped.

He stepped forward, closing the gap between us, and wrapped his bare hands around my flaming wrists.

"If I were lying, I'd be dead right now. Your fire would have killed me. You were counting on that when you jumped in that circle." His face was only inches from mine. "But you weren't planning for me to hear you. You expected a weaker demon—"

"You don't know what you're talking about," I hissed, struggling against the rage and the fire and the passion as they threatened to consume us both.

"You shot me and ran. I did the only thing I could to find you. I tracked down every member of the Antares Coven and questioned them. I made Kenneth du Lac sing before I ended him. He told me who you are, and how you were made, and why you're after him. I couldn't allow him to walk free after that. Not after knowing what he'd done to you."

I stood frozen, unable to even pull away. The silence between us was only broken by our breathing and the pulse of music from the club beyond.

"The magic you possess would kill anything on this earth, and in most other realms—except me. It hurts, but I don't truly burn. Why is that, Piper?"

My lips pressed together.

No. This was not happening. It wasn't *possible*.

I might not be fully human anymore, but I was human enough.

I refused to believe otherwise.

"I don't know who you are, but if I can't kill you, I'll find a way to send you back to the hell you came from."

He chuckled. "The only way I'm returning to where I came from is with you by my side."

"Not happening."

He leaned forward, closing the gap between us.

His lips brushed mine. I quivered, not from fear, but from fury.

His tongue darted out, sweeping the length of one of my fangs.

A growl rumbled through his chest, and I knew it was because of my blood.

I snapped my teeth at him, but he didn't move away.

He let me.

Shock filtered through as my fangs punctured his bottom lip. Magical ichor welled. Flavor exploded on my tongue and I saw stars as my blood quickened. I trembled with desire.

His hands loosened around my wrists, then skated down my arms to my shoulders, around my back. The hard pads of his fingers pressed into the sides of my breasts as he ran his splayed hands down either side of my body, stopping only to grip my hips. He pulled me flush against him, and I reached up, twining my own fingers in his hair.

A low moan built in my throat as I sucked on his bottom lip.

He hissed in pleasure, and his hands tightened. Nails pricked my skin, the tiny dose of pain just enough to break the trance.

As quickly as hunger took me, an icy cold washed over.

I pulled away, and his heated gaze tracked the movement.

Crimson dotted his lips, his own fangs were prominent and on display.

The door to the club blew open. A gust of wind that didn't belong shot straight for us. I slammed into the wall behind me while the demon was thrown across the room and into the pile of bodies on the bed.

"Come on!" The shout pulled at my attention.

Nathalie stood in the doorway with Barry at her side. The fae-witch hybrid had his eyes screwed shut in concentration as his hand movements directed the great wind, allowing me to pass.

With one look over my shoulder toward the figure slumped on the bed, I bolted out of the room. The door slammed shut behind me. Nathalie grabbed my hand, and before my head had righted itself, we were sprinting down the walkway toward the stairs.

"We're never going to make it," I panted as we ran as fast as our legs would carry us, pushing past the unsuspecting supes as they tried to get into the upper lounge.

"Not with that attitude, we won't," Nathalie quipped back.

What she didn't know was the rage in me was dulling. My reserve of power had only just recuperated, and the crash would be on me again within the hour. Less than, if the buzzing in my head was anything to go by.

I had to be back at my apartment before that happened.

I released her hand, using my enhanced strength to push myself harder, faster. I shoved patrons out of the way, clearing a way toward the door.

Behind us, a roar blasted through the club, making every supernatural stand to attention.

Nathalie winced.

"You shouldn't have come back for me," I said, shoving a couple out of the way. The door was only feet from us, and the calming magic of the club was gnawing at me. It hit already sensitive nerves, and if

12

RONAN

She ran. Again.

However, I wasn't angry. No. Not after I'd seen her past. The man she called Claude Lewis had tricked her. Lied to her. Ruined her.

I may have killed him and enjoyed it, but the damage was done. Piper hated magic and all magical beings, including me. She abhorred us for the atrocities committed against her and her people.

I might not have been in this world, or even known of her existence at the time, but it wouldn't matter to her. She blamed me with the rest of them, all the same.

Piper might have entered the first blood-exchange with me willingly, but I was going to have to tread carefully with her. Striking a fine balance between chasing her and giving her space.

She needed to grow. To heal. To learn that not every magical person would abuse or betray her.

I stared at the spot where the taxi had been. I could see it in her glowing red eyes as they faded to violet. She was entering stasis. The magic she wielded was wild. Unruly. Untamable. Yet . . . she'd tamed it. She bent it to her indomitable will, even if it robbed her of her strength afterward.

My atma was a strong woman, but for a time she would be weak.

Weak enough to find.

I stepped back into the shadows of the building behind me. A void blacker than night wrapped around me as I used my magic to traverse space itself, and I reappeared in the penthouse I'd taken. It had been one of Kenneth's before he signed over everything he owned to me.

I walked to the bar and poured myself a splash of scotch, then swirled the glass around to watch the honey-colored liquid coat the edge.

A buzzing built in the back of my head. It was almost time.

I swallowed the contents in a single motion. It had a smoky flavor, a hint of salt, yet smooth. A faint warmth followed it as I set the glass back on the counter and took a seat in the armchair before the fireplace. I had been watching the flickering flames when Greta MacArthur's mind brushed against mine, notifying me of Piper's arrival. I'd left her alive specifically to lure out my atma. The rest of the Antares Coven was already dead. Their money and estates all belonged to me now.

As well as their power, not that they had much.

All twelve members combined were no more than a single drop of what Piper held.

Then again, no being on this plane could compare to her. Not that she saw it. She handled her problems with firearms and a mean right elbow, even though she could end them all.

The buzzing turned to a burning.

I leaned back and never closed my eyes, though the penthouse faded from me. Flashes of memories replaced it. Images of a little blonde girl hiding under her bed, thinking if she couldn't see them, maybe the monsters wouldn't come. An older version of the same girl, shooting a firearm for the first time. Her hands shook, but they didn't shake when it showed her killing a vampire only two years later. She was twelve.

I watched from the shadows of her mind as Piper relived her past. She must have entered the stasis, and this is where it brought her. While these memories couldn't be relied upon to be exact, they still provided insight into the woman I sought.

For a long time, I didn't want an atma. I hoped I'd never find them. That perhaps fate would be kind to me for once and not give me one. But as the years went on, the strain of my magic became harder to contain, and I found myself searching.

Then actively hunting.

When the door opened up in front of me, I jumped through without looking back.

And when I saw her, standing in the circle, glaring at me with feverish blue eyes and blood stains on her face—she was not what I expected.

I needed her, regardless of her prejudice, but the desire to possess her, keep her, *own* her—I did not plan for that, and yet I felt it all the same. She called to me on more levels than one, and like the selfish god I was, I refused to deny myself.

It was for that reason alone that I finally stepped out of the shadows and put her nightmares to rest.

The walls broke apart into dust-like particles. The monsters trying to kill her paused, their faces going blank, before they vaporized. The furniture turned to nothing, and when there was only the ground left, that, too, dissipated.

Her mind went quiet as nothingness settled in around us.

Then she stiffened and squinted into the darkness, right where I stood.

She could sense me.

This woman, whom fate deemed insignificant, could sense me when no other could. She was my equal in every way.

Yet, she hated me.

I smiled cruelly and stepped out of the shadows.

"I TOLD you I'd find you," a voice said.

Ice ran through my veins.

He was here.

A dry, humorless chuckle slid from my lips. Of course he was here. This was my nightmare, after all. My price that I paid for the unholy magic that I allowed to ravage my body.

"You're nothing but a dream. A figment of my imagination," I said, turning around. The words dried up on my tongue when I looked at Ronan. He'd seated himself on a chair, ornate enough to be nothing less than a throne. His legs were crossed, ankle resting on top of his thigh. He leaned back, appraising me.

"Is that so?" he asked, running one of his hands over his stubbled jaw.

I didn't like his tone, or what it implied.

"Yes," I answered, and it sounded stronger than I felt. A hint of doubt wormed its way through me at the knowing tone he used. It shouldn't have. I shouldn't have thought twice because demons were liars, and this was my psyche . . .

But something made me consider it.

I didn't like the implications.

Ronan smiled, and it was incredibly cold and cruel, but also amused. There was a challenge in his steel-colored eyes. A purpose in his calloused hands.

He uncrossed his leg and leaned forward to stand. The throne disappeared behind him as he strode forward to stop before me.

"Then you won't mind if I do this—" He reached for me, his fingers brushing a strand of blonde hair away. They trailed down my face, around the curve of my cheek, and came to grip my chin. I flinched when he tilted my face up. He didn't seem that bothered by my reaction.

"Actually," I bit out, despite his grip. "I do." I turned my face away, and he let me.

He let me.

I cursed. Because that only aided those suspicions that this wasn't a dream.

At least not completely.

"The magic exacts this price on you because you

are unbalanced. Divided. The consequences will only get worse," Ronan started.

"You know this how?"

"I have seen your past."

"My past is not my future," I replied, stepping away.

"No," he agreed. "Your future will be worse because you are not human, Piper. You think you know things, but if you truly understood, you would not continue to run from me. I can be your salvation, but you will be *our* damnation if you do not let me."

My lips parted. He'd have shocked me less if he'd slapped me.

"If you know so much, then you'd know better than to chase. You'd know that whatever fascination you have with me is hopeless. I'm not your atma. I'm not your *anything*." I spat the words at him, but Ronan was unperturbed.

"That is where you are wrong," he said softly. "Your prejudice blinds you, and I can understand it— to an extent. After what happened to you . . . I can be a patient man because you are *everything*. Or you will be. If I have to chase you for a thousand years, I will. The magic does not lie. People do. And you, Piper"— he stepped forward once more, crowding my space —"you're the biggest liar of them all."

I shuddered because deep down, I knew.

He was telling the truth.

Ronan grinned like he knew it too.

"I'll be watching, Atma."

He stepped away.

"Wait," I bit out harshly. I hated this. I didn't want to do it, but I had to know.

Ronan paused. He lifted one dark eyebrow in silent question.

"If you are not one of my nightmares, then how are you here?"

His jaw tightened, and then he confirmed my worst suspicions.

"The blood-exchange. I took a piece of you, and you took a piece of me."

Then, just like the walls and the people and the floor before him, he disappeared.

I blinked, turning in circles, but Ronan was gone.

Not for good, though. Oh no. This wasn't over.

I had a feeling it was just getting started.

———

THE FIRST THING I registered as the crash wore off was the way sleep clung to me like a fog, trying to pull me under. I didn't fight it. Instead, I lay there, letting it pass through me as I slowly inched toward the surface.

It was only when cool fingers brushed over my forehead that I was able to open my eyes.

The light was muted. Dim. My skin felt hot and aching, like the remnants of a fever that had finally broken. I swallowed hard and then winced. My throat was dry; the tissue lining had cracked as if sandpaper had been scraped over it.

"Here," a voice said. I was too tired to be startled by the presence at my side. It should have registered when the fingers were touching, taking my temperature, I now realized.

But that was the crash for you. There was a reason I never let it happen in public.

Before now.

A glass of water appeared in front of me.

I sat up to drink it, reaching out with trembling hands. The cup shook in my tight grip as I brought it to my lips.

The crisp coolness hit my tongue, and I tipped my head back, swallowing as much as I could.

The cup emptied far too quickly, but when I swallowed this time, it didn't hurt so much. I counted that as a win, slowly lowering it from my face as the events before the crash came back to me.

"Fuck," I groaned. My hand dropped to my lap, and I took a sweep of the room.

My surprise must have shown on my face when I realized it was *my* room because Nathalie said, "Eidetic memory, remember? When you lost consciousness, I told the driver to bring us to the diner and from there I backtracked it to your apartment. I figured it was probably the safest place for us, given the bomb you have strapped to the door entrance."

"You stayed." Her words were still processing, but that was all I seemed to come up with when I searched for a response.

"I did, not that your utterly charming and grateful personality helped," she said sarcastically, running a pale hand through her light brown hair. My eyes raked over her, carefully noting the clean scent, fresh clothes, and slightly red nose.

"You also went through my apartment," I added, my voice slightly harder. There was a dangerous edge to it, reflecting the growing unease as I pulled myself out of the stupor the crash left me in.

Nathalie pursed her lips together. "You were unconscious, and I couldn't wake you. If I hadn't seen it last time, I would have thought you were violently ill."

"That's not a good excuse for going through my apartment," I said, even as some of the initial ire faded. She wasn't wrong, but given how well the new clothes fit, she'd also crossed a line whether or not she knew it.

"I have a cold, so I took the medicine you gave me before. I used the same shower and the same towel. I figured you'd rather I didn't wear your clothes, so I went looking in the other room—"

"Which is the problem," I said, flinging the covers aside.

"Well you weren't awake to tell me otherwise, so forgive my snooping for the basic necessities. I did get you out of there, you know," Nathalie said, getting to her feet to give me some room.

"I didn't ask you to," I snapped.

Tossing one leg over the side of the bed, I noticed that she'd also stripped me of my shoes and jeans before putting me to bed.

"Would it kill you to say thank you for once?" Nathalie groused, crossing her arms over her chest.

I reached out and put a hand on the edge of my nightstand, using it to brace myself as I stood. I grabbed my pants and pulled them on, strapping my holster to my thighs as well. I looked to the clock and the glowing red letters read 1:15 in the afternoon.

I gritted my teeth.

"How long have I been out?"

At that, she didn't answer right away. I had to work to control the panic inside me as I took in her guarded expression. She looked away, a guilty twist of her lips confirming it.

"How long?" I repeated in barely more than a whisper.

"Two and a half days."

The ground nearly dropped out from under me.

I tripped as I moved forward, and then brushed

past her. My living room barely registered as I stumbled toward the front door.

"What are you doing?" Nathalie called as I peered through the tiny circle window in the center.

"Has anyone come to the door?"

"What?" she asked, like that was a crazy thought. "No, no one's been at the door."

"Have you seen anyone lurking outside?" I demanded.

"No, I haven't seen anyone 'lurking' outside."

I glanced over my shoulder at the tone in her voice. "You think I'm being paranoid."

She scanned my features and then sighed. "It's been quiet. No one's come to the door. When I left to get groceries, no one followed me—"

"Are you sure?" I asked her. If I were someone else, I might have thought I was just a little paranoid.

Given who my boss was—or ex-boss, I should say—I wasn't taking my chances.

"Yes," Nathalie sighed. "I did a tracking spell both on the way there and back since you have a demon on your trail."

"By your own admission, your magic isn't consistent. Are you *one hundred percent positive* that no one followed—"

"Yes, Piper. I'm sure," she groaned, turning on her heel to enter the kitchen.

I stepped away from the door, and slowly trailed

back into the living room, narrowing my eyes on her. She drifted toward one of the cabinets and pulled out a glass, then moved to get herself water before going for the package of cold medicine that was on the counter.

"My boss will have heard that the Antares Coven has been taken out. He probably knows it wasn't me that did it, and we have less than twelve hours before my three days is up. Of those three, I've been unconscious for most of them, and you've been in and out of my apartment—so forgive me for being a little fucking paranoid when the people I used to work for tend to send assassins *before* they put a price on a head." I raised my voice toward the end of my speech because truth be told, I was feeling more than a little unraveled after the week I'd had.

Nathalie didn't react, though. Not the way she should have. If anything, she seemed unbothered by my anger.

"Are you done yet?" she asked in a bored tone while making a sandwich.

Annoyance and anger sizzled through me.

"Are you always so lax with safety?" I asked her, tilting my head. My heartbeat picked up a fraction, but it wasn't anywhere near dangerous levels. Yet. "Because if I didn't know any better . . . I'd say you simply don't care. And for someone that *begged* to work with me so that you could keep your ass alive,

I'm starting to wonder why you keep putting yourself in positions that do the opposite. In fact, working with me at all doesn't lend to staying safe. Which makes me wonder, why are you here?"

She paused, lifting her head. I could tell that she only just realized where I was going with this.

"I'm not working for your boss," she said quietly. "And I know you don't really think that, or you'd have killed me already."

"You're a good liar," I said. "A great one. You use subtle manipulations to play people. I watched you do it with that McArthur bastard. How do I know you haven't been playing me? That you're not waiting for the call to be put out just to kill me where I stand?"

Nathalie sighed and then lowered her eyes, before raising them to meet mine.

"Because I want to work with you—" she started.

"Why?" I bit out. "You've yet to really give me an answer. Your coven excommunicated you, yes, but you could have found a new one. I bet Barry would have taken you in, or worst case—you could have left. But you're dead set on staying with me. On helping me. I need to know why, right now, or we're going to have a problem."

Maybe I was a tiny bit paranoid. It was possible.

But things simply weren't adding up. For a girl that wanted to live so much, she latched onto the person who literally kidnapped her—then wouldn't leave me when I told her to—it just didn't make sense. Survival of the fittest.

No one was that loyal. And from the time I'd spent with her, I knew she wasn't stupid.

If anything, she was smarter than she let on.

"Okay," she said. Her shoulders slumped as she set down the knife she'd used to smear peanut butter and jelly on bread. "I'll tell you why. I haven't been completely honest with you." When my jaw tightened, she gave me a hard look. "You don't get to judge given you kidnapped me, haven't told me shit about what you are or why the demon wants you, not to mention the fact that I got us back here on my own—"

"Spit it out."

"I'm not a gray witch."

I blinked. "Then what are you?"

"I don't know," she said. "I have magic, but not like my family's magic. Everything I told you about my magic was true, but I don't have a color align-ment. I *do* have an ability, though. When I touch someone for the first time, I see . . . things about them." She struggled for words. "Sometimes it's just a feeling for who they are. Sometimes I get visions of the future. Their future. It's different every time."

"All right," I said, running a hand through my hair. I walked up to the other side of the counter and leaned one hip against it. "So you're some kind of witch freak. Not the weirdest thing I've seen or heard. What's it got to do with me?"

"When we touched the first time, I had a premonition I've never had before. It was like a feeling, but more—and before you ask, no, I don't really know how to explain it better than that. It told me you're my future. You. Singularly. That I will find my way because of you—and that any future without you ends in death."

"That's an awful lot to get from a backhand," I pointed out.

"This ability—whatever it is—it's never wrong. Believe me, when I first woke up and you were tying me to a chair, I really wished it were otherwise."

I let out a heavy exhale. "Were you lying to me about anything else?"

"No," she said.

"Is there any way for me to confirm that?"

A slight grin curled around her lips. "Unfortunately for you, a blood oath or a spell are the only ways. Given I don't think you can cast spells, pretty sure that only leaves the oath. Something I'm not so sure you want to do with your aversion to magic . . ."

She wasn't wrong. I really didn't like the idea of any kind of binding . . . but I also liked the idea that she was actually a bounty hunter, or worse, an assassin working for my boss, even less. My dislike of magic came from the price of it. Not many things were worse than being dead, though.

The real question was, did I trust her more than I hated magic?

Or did I trust magic more than her?

"What's the price of the blood oath?"

She didn't even blink. "Whatever you ask of it, you also have to give. So, in this case, if you want truth, I'll also be allowed to ask for truth. If either of us lies, it kills us both."

Motherfucker.

Of course it would have a built-in equalizer. How fucking convenient.

I'd have my answers, but only if I were willing to offer up my own truths.

"If what you say is true, you have no intention of leaving at any point, do you?"

"Nope," she said, taking a bite of her sandwich. "Even if you try to make me. I told you, I don't want to die, and the only way that's going to happen is if I stick around with you."

Fuck me.

"You know, all of this would be a lot simpler if I just shot you."

I pulled one of my guns out of my holster, weighing it in my hand. She lifted her eyebrows in question, but she didn't look afraid.

"You won't," she said, then shrugged and went

back to eating her sandwich.

"What makes you so sure?"

She gave me a dubious look and set her sandwich back down. Nathalie walked around the kitchen, reaching up to brush the crumbs from the side of her mouth as she did so.

"If I wasn't confident in my ability, I wouldn't be here," she started, coming to stand directly in front of me. She reached out with narrow fingers and curled my own around the handle of the gun.

I squinted, not sure where this was going. Then she lifted that hand and pressed the end of the barrel to her forehead.

I'd thought she was smart.

I was starting to wonder if I should have questioned if she was crazy.

"You truly believe that I won't shoot you," I said softly.

"If you're going to, get it over with. If you want the blood oath, fine, let's do this. But we're more likely to die from you not trusting me when we both need you to. So make up your mind, Piper." She released the barrel and lowered her arms, letting me hold the gun aimed at her forehead.

We stood there, staring at each other.

I'd be lying if I didn't say part of me was tempted to just do it. If she truly planned on sticking around, there was no way she wouldn't eventually find out the truth. Not to mention the complications of having a partner with me for the foreseeable future. I'd worked alone for so long now that I no longer knew what it was like to work with someone.

But something stopped me.

She stood up to Ronan and said no. Whatever her reasons, no hired help would do that. And if I were being honest with myself, I was pretty sure she was telling the truth this time.

I re-holstered the gun.

"The rules still stand. You get one shot to fuck up and then I end you."

"Glad to know this changed nothing," she noted dryly.

Whatever I was going to say was cut off as a knock came at the door.

We both stilled, exchanging a cautious glance.

"I'm going to answer the door," I said, speaking quietly. "Get behind the island and don't use magic offensively, even if you're in danger."

"You got it," Nathalie said, going to stand back behind the kitchen counter. She took another bite of her sandwich, waving me on when I gave her a peeved look.

I shook my head and walked silently to the door, careful to avoid the floorboard that creaks. My better hearing was picking up on the sounds of breathing coming from the hallway.

It was too erratic to be only one person.

I leaned forward, hovering over the eyehole into the hallway.

The barrel of a gun stared me down on the other side.

I barely had time to jump away from the door before a shot went off, followed by an explosion.

Flames consumed the front entrance to my apartment. I pulled myself up onto my elbows and then rolled onto my side.

Three bodies lay dead outside.

Hitmen.

I recognized one of them as Ronny. His face was angled to the side and blood dripped from his ears and nose. Silver shards stuck out from his face. The explosive bomb I had rigged to my door did its job.

I swallowed hard.

"I take it these are the assassins you were expecting?" Nathalie asked, her voice sounding too close to be coming from the kitchen. I glanced over my shoulder to see her standing only two feet away, face grim as she stared at the dead men. Or what was left of them.

"You would be correct."

I got to my feet and approached the three.

Anders knew my record, which meant my boss did as well. This wasn't a true hit. They expected me to kill these men. That's why they sent Ronny. I liked him. Not romantically, but still more than I should have. Enough that I had to hide the wince every time my eyes grazed over his prone form.

This was a warning.

My time was up.

There was now a price on my head.

14

"We need to get out of here," I said, turning away from the gaping hole where my front door should have been. Good thing I hadn't paid the electric bill this week. "If my boss gave the order, Anders won't have any qualms about handing out this address. We probably don't have more than an hour before bounty hunters will be crawling all over the place."

I was already starting for my room when Nathalie put her hand on my arm.

Before I could get annoyed, she said, "What do you need me to do?"

I looked her over. A decade of prejudice warring against the unyielding loyalty she'd given me. Loyalty I didn't deserve.

"In my room under the bed there's a backpack

and a duffel bag already packed. Grab them both, we need to be out of here in the next five."

She nodded once and went to grab the packs. I took a deep breath and turned for the second room. The one I avoided more than I should.

The handle turned easily, and the door swung open without much effort at all. It was clean to the point of almost sterile. Light blue walls with faded paint and a chipped white dresser with a twin bed were the only things giving it life. That and the twenty-three-year-old woman sleeping in it.

Her long brown hair splayed across the pillow in perfect, even waves. She never rolled or turned, so it stayed that way. Grease clung to the roots around her scalp from too long between washings. Her pale skin was even and smooth, but dry and unnaturally white from not seeing the light of day in so long. Her eyes were closed. Peaceful. A necklace hung from her neck, the thin silver chain unbreakable. It held a singular stone over the hollow of her throat that pulsed faintly. The magic in it was all that kept her alive. It prevented her body from wasting away and muscle atrophy from kicking in.

Guilt ate at me as I grabbed clothes out of the dresser. I knelt before her and pushed the sheet back, then dressed her in the most clinical way possible. I'd done this for long enough that it was almost second nature to take care of her in this way. To manipulate her limbs like that of a doll. To dress and clean and carry her because she couldn't do any of that for herself anymore.

I was just finishing braiding her hair when a quiet voice at the door said, "I got the bags."

"Good," I said, focusing on picking up the limp body before me. She was heavier than she used to be, and lighter than she should be. I stood up, and whatever Nathalie thought, it didn't show on her face. "Let's go."

She nodded once, and we were off.

I didn't glance at the dead bodies as I stepped over them. I didn't look back at the place I'd called home for as long as I could remember. I held the unconscious girl to my chest and carried on.

As we descended the steps, Nathalie said, "I get the feeling that we're not just venturing out. Do you have a place in mind?"

"I do."

"I don't suppose you'll tell me where," she continued nonchalantly as I stepped off the stairwell. Instead of walking out the front door, I turned to a metal door with peeling gray paint and a rusted handle.

"You'll see if we manage to get there without dying."

I adjusted my grip to lean into the door and used my elbow to turn the lever. It squeaked, echoing up the corridor. Nathalie looked up, but no one opened their door to look. I kicked back and the metal frame resisted but failed as I freed the lock from the latch. It opened and hit the wall behind it with a bang. Fluorescent lights flickered, trying to power on and illuminate the underground parking garage. Nathalie peered through the doorway, then gave me a questioning look.

Instead of answering, I started down one of the rows. The door screeched as it closed behind us. Nathalie's footsteps followed softly at my heels.

"Nice place you got here," she said slowly.

While it was filled with cars, they were mostly trashed and outdated. Windows were shattered. Tires slashed. Words had been spray-painted on the scratched and dented metal. What survived the collapse of the American government and subsequent Magic Wars didn't survive the years of wear and tear that followed. While some factories that made cars still existed, they were few and far between—not to mention expensive.

We'd reverted back to a time when vehicles were a luxury for the filthy rich, or those lucky enough to have one still running from before the wars. Like me.

I came to a stop at the end of the parking garage, in front of a beat-up Honda Civic. The tires were deflated or missing. The windows smashed. The leather interior ripped open and center console was destroyed. On the outside, the once cobalt blue paint was scratched and had been spray-painted over to read: Oppress the Oppressors. It was one mantra that had become popular during the Magic Wars, and a mindset that led to the downfall of humans being in power, despite their greater numbers.

I laid the girl in my arms on the trunk and then got on one knee to reach under the bumper. "What are you—" Nathalie started right as I found what I was looking for. I pressed each of my fingers to the cloaking device, going in a specific order and waiting three seconds in between. At the end of the sequence, the illusion dropped to reveal an old but well-maintained car. I stood up and went around to open the side door. The scent of pine faintly drifted over me. When I went back to pick up the girl, Nathalie gave me an appraising look.

"You hate magic," she said. Something squirmed inside me, but I ignored it as I carried the unconscious girl to the backseat and then buckled her in. Nathalie came to stand beside me. "But you use it sometimes."

"You got a point?" I asked sharply, testing the resistance on the seatbelt before standing back up and closing the door.

"More that I'm confused. For someone that distrusts it so much, you seem to use it whenever you need it. I can't tell if that makes you a hypocrite, or if

149

it just means you don't truly distrust it—you distrust the people who use it."

"Get in the car," I said, extending a hand and motioning to the duffel bag she had hanging at her side. Nathalie frowned, but lifted the strap over one shoulder and extended it.

I walked around to the driver's side and opened the back door, tossing the bag in the seat. I rifled through it, grabbing the set of keys, then closed it up and slammed the back door shut behind me. Nathalie was already in the passenger seat when I climbed in the front. She said nothing as I stuck the keys in the ignition and the engine turned over. After two tries, it spluttered to life. I breathed a tight sigh of relief and backed out of the spot.

It had been a while since I'd driven. My understanding of the controls was amateur at best, given I was never really well acquainted with it. My parents had said that kids would learn to drive at sixteen and they often have their own cars.

When I was sixteen, my parents were murdered, and the world had already gone to shit. This was their car, and it was really pure dumb luck that it was still running.

I pulled up to the gate of the parking garage. It had stopped working years ago when the rioting got so bad the residents were concerned they'd bring the building down. Someone smashed the receiver box, and since then, the only way to open it was manually.

I put the car in park. "I need you to get out and open the gate."

"I'd ask if you're going to drive off without me, but I suspect you'd probably give me the same answer either way."

My lips twitched. A grin threatening to break through.

Nathalie got out of the car and went to hoist the gate up. It took her the better part of a minute to even lift it high enough the car could get underneath. I slowly rolled onto the street and stopped before turning.

She slipped out from under the gate.

The heavy metal hit the pavement with a loud crack.

Heads turned, and I shot them a cool look as I waited the ten seconds for her to run back to the passenger side and hop in. The door wasn't even closed before I started driving.

Only when a few minutes had passed—and I still didn't see any sign of someone following us—did I relax enough to speak. "I'm not sure whether or not I'm a hypocrite. I hate magic, but because of the world we live in, sometimes I'm forced to use it—and I hate that too. But when the choice is between dying or using it, I'll choose to live."

I sensed Nathalie's eyes watching me, but I kept my own on the road. It was hard enough to drive even when I was paying full attention.

"Why do you hate it?" she asked.

I couldn't help looking in the rearview mirror at the unconscious girl.

She was a woman now, but in my mind, she'd always be a girl.

"All magic has a price, and some of us don't want to pay it," I said. It was the same thing I'd told Anders a week ago.

"All that really means is you paid too much," Nathalie replied, leaning against the passenger window. "What's her name?"

"What?"

"The girl in the back," she said, motioning behind us.

I pressed my lips together.

"Seriously? You can be exasperating sometimes," she said, shaking her head.

"I could still shoot you," I reminded her. She snorted, and I frowned.

"We both know you won't. I gave you the chance, and you didn't take it. You're stuck with me," she said. I wrinkled my nose at that, flipping the turn signal on to get on the highway.

"Like fungus," I muttered.

Nathalie snorted again, running her hand over her mouth to cover her grin.

"I think you like me."

"You can be useful," I said. Her expression turned sour.

"Come on. Is it really that hard to admit?" she said, jesting. "Piper Fallon, witch hunter extraordinaire, likes a witch?"

Whatever traces of a grin I might have been fighting faded as I murmured, "Yes."

Nathalie leaned back, crossing her arms. "Why?" she asked, also turning serious. She didn't seem offended by my small truth, just curious.

"Because . . ." I breathed. "Witches took everything from me."

15

Nathalie blinked. Her lips parted. I focused on the road, a grim set to my jaw.

"When you say everything—"

"I mean everything," I cut in, my voice hard. She wrinkled her nose and seemed to think on that while I drove.

After a few minutes, she said, "Well that just sucks."

Going against everything I knew about driving, I looked away from the road. Her face was sincere, even if her words weren't the usual standard party line I'd heard.

I'm sorry for your loss.

My condolences.

Not all witches are bad.

The list of things I'd heard over the years went on

and on, each one more infuriating than the last. But I could honestly say that no one had dared to just call it like it was.

"Yeah," I said slowly, turning back to the road. "It does suck." I had to jerk us back between the lanes, and if Nathalie had thoughts about my driving, she smartly kept them to herself.

We drove the rest of the way in comfortable silence. It wasn't exactly far where we were going; just far enough to put some distance between us and the people hunting us. Far enough that I could think without my door being blown off.

I pulled off the mostly deserted highway. Two rights and a left put us on a poorly paved back road. I followed it down till the pavement crumbled and then kept driving. At the end of the line, a dirt road took off into the woods where a somewhat kept driveway used to be. Branches scratched the top of the car as I slowed to a crawl, knowing where to drive only from memory. Vines and grass had grown where there used to be dirt. Trees towered on either side of the long drive. We pushed through the worst of it, and when it was only dead grass between us and the cabin, I parked and cut the engine.

Cities weren't as loud as they'd once been. New Chicago certainly wasn't. While the wind still blew, the lack of sirens, fewer vehicles, and fewer people made it quieter. Seedier.

Still, it was nothing like being in the true wilderness. The sun peeked through breaks in the canopy, and the birds chirped as I stepped out of the old Honda.

Memories from the last time I was at the cabin danced in front of my eyes.

It had been the summer before I turned sixteen.

"You okay?" Nathalie asked, coming to stand beside me.

I took a deep breath and turned away from those memories. It was the past, and it needed to stay there. "Yeah, I'm fine."

I opened the back door and threw the duffel bag over one shoulder, and then went around to the other side to grab the unconscious woman. Her head lolled against my shoulder as I carried her toward the cabin. The steps creaked under my boots, but they held firm as I climbed up to the wraparound porch.

This house didn't have any kind of magical lock, and the shitty turnkey one it had we'd never bothered with. With magic in the world, my father didn't see the point in locking it. If someone wanted to get in, they would. And anyone else could just smash the windows or break down the door. It was better to keep it open and hope they took whatever they were after, leaving the place without destroying it.

I hoped that after ten years it was still intact, though I had my doubts.

Shuffling the girl to one side, I leaned against the door and used the side of my hand to turn the knob. The door opened with an eerie creak.

The blinds were closed, and the generator wasn't on yet, but just from what little light came through the doorway, I could make out the living area. A couch and two oversized armchairs sat on top of an antique rug. A chipped coffee table rested in the middle.

I stepped inside, noting how it was all there, the same way we'd left it.

It was the only thing that was the same a decade later.

"Where are we?" Nathalie asked, coming up behind me.

"My family's cabin."

I laid the girl down on the couch and walked around the back of it. A small dining area with a circular wooden table and four chairs sat in front of the sliding back door. I pushed the thick drapes aside, letting the afternoon sun shine through.

While everything was covered in an inch of dust, it was completely undisturbed.

"There's no food here," Nathalie said from the kitchen. She had all the cabinets open and was peering into one when I looked over at her.

"Even if there was, it wouldn't be good by now. We'll make do with what I brought."

She sighed, closing up the cabinets. "Is there a bathroom here?"

"Straight down the hall," I said without turning. "You'll want to run the tap for a few minutes to clear the pipes. And don't drink it. It's well water, but who knows what's in it now."

When the bathroom door clicked shut, I opened the back door and stepped outside. Following the porch around to the side, I knelt in front of the generator, hoping it still worked. The fuel valve turned on without an issue, but the choke rod was stiff. After a few attempts, I got it. The silence in the wintry forest started to creep in as the branches rustled.

So quiet . . .

It was unsettling how the lack of noise snuck beneath the skin, like an itch that couldn't be scratched. Or really, noise operated as a distraction. Without it, there was a void where uncertainty and fear could slink in.

I glanced out at the forest, but there was nothing there. Nothing but dried leaves and barren branches. The sun filtered through the trees, casting long shadows that were growing longer by the minute. I shook my head and turned back to the generator, flipping the ignition switch on. I pulled the recoil cord, and it emitted a loud hum. It was a softer sound than a car engine, but still loud in the dead of winter.

I moved the choke to *run* and waited a moment to

make sure nothing funny happened. When the hum continued, I got to my feet and dusted myself off. A cold wind blew by, whipping my braid across my face. I flicked it back and went inside.

"We need to talk," Nathalie said, as I closed the sliding door behind me.

I strode past her, over to the fireplace. The red bricks were smudged black with soot, and the metal rods inside that held the wood up were rusted. "About?" I asked, peering inside and up the chimney.

"Why are we here?" she asked. I squinted past my reflex to sneeze. A faint light shone from the top, which meant it was unblocked. Good. It was fucking freezing.

"In case you haven't noticed, my apartment door was blown off by assassins," I said, lowering my head again to pull myself out of the chimney.

Nathalie grumbled something under her breath before saying, "I'm aware of the assassins. Why are we *here?*"

"Because it's safe."

"It's in the middle of nowhere. Assuming no one followed us or can track us, which is a terrible assumption by the way, there's not enough food in the duffel bag to last us more than three days. I know because I checked. And before you say, 'well I can hunt,' I don't want to live off of squirrel for the winter—"

"For one, I can't hunt. I was born and raised in

New Chicago. While my family came out here for a couple of weeks every summer, we weren't survivalists. We were—" I broke off and let out a tight breath. "It doesn't matter. The point is this is temporary. We're only going to be here for the night. I needed somewhere I could keep her while I dealt with my old boss. We'll be gone in the morning. So get comfortable. I'm going to chop us some wood."

"You're going to deal with your boss?"

"I don't have a choice," I replied.

"There's always a choice," she said.

"Dealing with him or dying. I've still got things to take care of, so dying isn't an option."

"You could run," she suggested.

I shook my head. "He'd find me no matter where I went, and he won't give up. Not when he thinks I betrayed him. I have to face this."

She didn't respond immediately, and I took that as my cue to start for the back door again.

"Piper?" Nathalie said, before I could leave.

"What?"

"I'm sorry about your sister," she said softly.

My head whipped back, but she wasn't looking at me. She was looking at the sleeping woman on the couch.

I wasn't sure how she put it together, but I didn't ask. It didn't really matter because it was the truth.

"Her name was—is . . . Bree."

I opened the back door and stepped outside into the cold.

Nathalie didn't follow.

IT WAS after dark when I returned.

The light on the back porch flickered in and out, the yellow luminescence calling me back. I reached for the backdoor handle, noticing then how white my fingers were. Red blotches stained my hands. If I had a mirror, I'd bet my cheeks were also the same ruddy shade after hours outside chopping wood. The two logs I carried under my arm were just a small amount compared to the pile I'd left in the woods.

The back door opened with a shrill squeal.

I frowned when I saw Nathalie standing on the opposite side of the kitchen with her arms crossed over her chest. A white paper plate with a sandwich sat in the middle of the table. I wasn't sure if this was her idea of bargaining power or a truce.

I shut the sliding door behind me, cutting off the worst of the screaming winds.

"You were out for quite a while," she said, her eyes dropping to the two logs.

"Needed time to think," I said, striding past the table toward the fireplace. She stepped in front of me and extended both hands.

"Let me. You go eat."

I lifted an eyebrow and handed her the wood. She shooed me toward the table with a look. As I took a seat at one of the rickety wooden chairs, sweat started to practically pour off of me. I grimaced, pulling at the turtleneck.

"So," Nathalie started nonchalantly. "What's the plan for tomorrow?"

"You didn't have to do all this to ask me that," I said, taking a bite of the peanut butter and jelly sandwich.

She grunted as she finished maneuvering the logs and then looked up and wiped a stray brown lock from her forehead. "I made you a sandwich," she said skeptically. "Also, you aren't exactly the most forthcoming with information. You wouldn't even tell me where we were going until we got here." She motioned to the cabin.

I nodded while I chewed. "If we didn't make it out of the city, I didn't want the information tortured out of you."

To her credit, she didn't pale or even outwardly react as she set to work with the can of lighter fluid and match sticks. It took her three attempts to get it, but when she was done, an orange fire glowed, casting the room in warm shadows. "Why can you tell me your plans now, then?" she said. She got up and came to sit in the chair across from me.

"Knowledge is power. If you're planning to come with me tomorrow, which I assume you are, then you need to know what you're up against. Ignorance could get us both killed." I set half of my sandwich down and leaned back to read her face.

She was grinning.

I frowned.

"You've decided to trust me."

"I've decided to not kill you," I corrected.

Nathalie snorted. "Whatever you need to tell yourself, Piper. I know the truth."

My chest squeezed a little bit because I knew the truth too—and she wasn't far off. A decade of life lessons told me I was stupid. That this decision was going to get me, and by extension my sister, killed. All my training, all those years, every single thing said I was going to regret this.

Except one.

My gut.

It was telling me a different story. Given Nathalie hadn't tried to kill me yet, I was trusting it. For now.

"My old boss is very powerful. He'll have bounty hunters all over the city looking for us. We'll have to be careful."

"Anders isn't your boss?" she asked, kicking her feet up on the wooden chair opposite of her. I shot her a look, and she immediately lowered them, grinning sheepishly.

"No," I rolled my eyes. "He was just the middle-man. Hiring hunters is beneath my actual boss. Anders was his paper pusher, and he handled the shit my boss deemed not worth his time."

Nathalie leaned forward, resting her elbows on the chipped wooden tabletop. She looked me square in the eye as she asked, "So *who* is your boss?"

"Lucifer."

Her brown eyes turned a slight shade of amber as she slumped back. "Lucifer?" she repeated. "He's your boss?" I nodded, and she let out a curse. "Well shit, no wonder I couldn't figure out who'd employed you after you left human patrol. With your hatred of magic, I never would have thought—"

"I never met him. It was only ever Anders I dealt with, but Lucifer paid twice as good as human patrol with half the rules. I got to choose who I hunted and how I brought them in." I shrugged, having lost my appetite to finish the sandwich despite chopping wood for hours. "The gig was good."

"Until now."

I nodded. "Until now."

She mulled that over for a moment before saying, "I didn't know he was in New Chicago."

"Most people don't," I shrugged. "I don't even know for certain he's here now, but I suspect he is."

"Why is that?"

"Two reasons." I held up one finger. "Paranoia."

I held up the second. "Technology. Those two go hand in hand for a demon. He'll be paranoid about anything he deems as his, and he'll want to oversee it himself to some degree, and he likely won't trust technology one bit. He's also cunning. He wouldn't want people to know he's here. For one as old as him to have never been caught, and still be ruling after all this time, he's gotta be in New Chicago more often than not. I suspect Anders reports to him personally."

"And if he's not?" she asked skeptically.

"We cross that bridge when we come to it."

Nathalie released a breath. "No wonder you were paranoid I was an assassin sent to kill you. You must have really wanted that information from the demon to be willing to gamble like this." It was subtle. A sly attempt at nudging the conversation that way. My lips tightened around one corner of my mouth.

"I do, yes."

Silence passed between us. Her gaze trying to prompt me to tell her, and my own flinty stare telling her not to go there.

"But it's not the most pressing issue right now," I added. "We need to take out Lucifer. Permanently."

Her eyebrows inched up her forehead. "How exactly do you plan to do that?"

"We're going to kidnap Anders and get his where-abouts from him," I said.

It was her turn to frown. "That's it?" she asked. "That's your plan?"

"Anders isn't the only one who knows how to track. I followed him home a few times. I know where he lives. We can get the drop on him undetected and then find Lucifer."

Nathalie put her hands up and then pressed her palms into her eyes. "You've got to be kidding me," she muttered to herself. She dropped her hands and gave me a serious look. "First, you're assuming Anders knows his location. He might, but that's a big *if*. Are you sure you want to bet on that?"

"I don't have a better plan to find him," I said. "It's not like there's a phone number I can look up to call and book an appointment. This guy is a *demon*, and he's a secretive one at that."

"Okay, assuming that Anders does know—which is an assumption, and not a good one—how do you plan to kill him? Do you even know how to kill a demon?"

I pressed my lips together.

"Oh my god. You don't know how to, do you?"

"I was planning to figure that out once I found him," I said in a tight voice.

"You can't just figure that out," she argued.

"Sure you can," I said, pulling one of my pistols from the holster at my hip to place it on the table. "He wouldn't be the first supe I've hunted without knowing how to kill them. I've figured it out with all the ones in the past. I can do it again."

"This isn't just a normal supe," Nathalie continued. "Demons don't even come from earth."

"I'm aware," I snapped.

"But you don't know how to kill him."

"I'll figure it out," I repeated in a hard voice. Part of the problem was that I did have a plan, or rather, a solution. I already knew bullets didn't work, but bullets weren't the only weapon in my arsenal. The white fire I created while in my other form would destroy pretty much anything. *Except Ronan.* I pushed that thought aside. Even Ronan said it could destroy almost anything. I had a feeling Lucifer counted.

But I wasn't planning on telling Nathalie that just yet.

"I vote we come up with a new plan," she said.

"You don't get a vote."

"Sure I do," she said dismissively. "We're both going to die when this fails, so we both get a vote. I vote to come up with another plan. A better one, where we don't die."

"You said yourself that you'll live as long as you stick with me."

"That doesn't mean I'm testing it," she said, throwing her hands up.

"Could have fooled me," I muttered, pushing away from the table.

"Where are you going?" she demanded as I got to my feet.

I motioned to myself. "In case you haven't noticed, I'm sweating my ass off right now. I need a shower."

Nathalie got to her feet to follow me. "Your shower can wait. We need a plan."

"We have a plan," I groaned. Talking to her was like talking to a brick wall.

"A new plan," she corrected.

"For fuck's sake," I snapped. "We have two objectives. Two. Find Lucifer. Kill Lucifer. The only contact I even have that *might* be in touch with him is Anders. It's a start. If it doesn't work, we come up with another plan and another plan and another plan —until it does."

"Lucifer isn't the only demon in the city," she said.

I stopped mid-step down the hall and turned to look at her.

"What?"

"I know you heard me. You hear better than any human. Lucifer isn't the only demon in the city—and he isn't the only demon after you. We can use that."

My tongue traced the edge of my teeth as I debated. Nathalie stood at the end of the hall, arms crossed and hip cocked. She leaned against the wall and tilted her head, a curtain of warm brown hair spilling over one shoulder.

"I'm listening."

She flashed me a Cheshire smile.

My heart dropped. I had a feeling that whatever plan she was concocting was going to make mine seem sane.

"One demon wants to kill you. The other has a vested *interest* in keeping you alive." She looked me up and down once as she said it.

"We don't know that," I said, the tone of my voice warning her.

Too bad she wasn't going to listen.

"Oh no," she laughed as she said the words. "Neither of us is stupid, Piper. You were alone in that room for ten minutes with him, and not a scratch was on you when Barry and I got you out. He might be hunting you, but he doesn't want you dead." She gave me a pointed look, and I rolled my eyes, trying to dismiss it even as my heart started to beat erratically.

"Maybe," I said apathetically, shrugging one shoulder.

"It doesn't matter *why* he wants you, but he does. Probably as much as the other one wants you dead. I vote we use that. Use *him*. Who better to kill a demon than another demon?"

The shit-eating grin on her face said she was pretty damn proud of herself.

I pressed my lips together, not wanting to praise

her further . . . because it was a good plan. Or at least the makings of one.

Instead, I took a step toward her, and motioned vaguely with one hand. "So tell me, how would we go about using one demon to kill the other?"

As impossible as it should have been, her smile widened.

My heart thumped again. Dread thickened in my gut.

"By doing what you do best," she said. I lifted a brow in question. "We lay a trap to lure our prey using just the right bait."

The look she gave me made her intention clear.

Me. I was the bait.

Goddamnit.

1 6

It was late by the time we finished hatching our plan, and by the end, it was *good*.

This was going to work.

It had to.

At least that's what I told myself as I laid down in the musty, old twin bed that smelled of cedar balls and cinnamon apples. I pulled the sheet up around my breasts and turned, flicking my wet hair behind me as I tried to get comfortable.

Despite the restlessness inside me, sleep wasn't hard to come by.

I knew it had come when I saw the flickering candlelight of a chandelier.

Church pews surrounded me, pushed to the side. A circle was drawn, and blood ran around the edges, but where it came from wasn't clear. There were no hooded figures this time. No athames. No chanting. If anything, it was eerily silent.

"I wondered how long it would be before you fell asleep," a voice said behind me. It was shadows and night. Winter skies and mercury. The sting of a knife pressed intimately to skin.

"Why are you here?" I asked, without turning to face him. I didn't want to look this time, cowardly as it may have been. Looking at him did things to me. It was painful and pleasurable, and I wanted no part.

"I told you last time," he said. I sensed him walking around the edge of the circle. Drawing near. Was he in it? Or outside of it? I wasn't sure.

"I didn't ask *how* you were here," I said, looking at the ceiling. "I asked why." It wasn't stained glass, but instead a painting. Or rather, many of them. Pictures of Christ and his angels. Of Mother Mary.

The world as we knew it didn't believe in a singular religion. That changed the day the president was killed by a witch on live television. All the faith in the world couldn't have saved him from it. The Secret Service was wiped out at the same time. One by one, supes became known, and before long, we learned that all these ancient deities were just supes that envisioned themselves as gods at some point in history.

Some still clung to faith, per se, but it had changed. They hoped if they worshipped these beings of magic, that perhaps they'd be spared from the cost.

Why did it always come down to the price?

"This was where you changed, was it not?" Ronan asked me, pulling me from my thoughts.

"That's a mild way to describe the life-altering event that occurred beneath these lifeless eyes," I said, both greedily and guiltily taking in every feature of the cathedral, including the portrait of Jesus I'd stared at when it happened. I had prayed then. Only a different god answered.

"How would you rather I say it?"

"I'd rather we didn't speak of it at all," I replied firmly.

He stepped into my periphery, still wearing a suit. His black hair had been pulled back into a low ponytail. Those swirling mists of chaos focused on me.

"Then why did you bring us here?" he asked softly.

"I didn't bring us anywhere," I replied, voice hard.

"On the contrary, this is your dream. When you sleep, the blood-exchange pulls me to you. I have no control over the location. So I ask you again, Atma, why did you bring us here if you'd rather we not speak of it?"

My mouth felt dry as I said, "Don't call me that."

"It's what you are."

He said it with conviction, as if he stated that the sky was blue and the mountains tall. If I were any less obstinate, I might have crumbled.

But I was Piper Fallon.

I did not crumble, buckle, or bend. Certainly not for a demon.

"Do you have to come to me when I sleep?" I asked him, changing directions. If he could tell I was deflecting, he didn't say anything.

"No."

"Then why do you?"

He moved directly in front of me, and I pointedly didn't look him in the face, instead opting to stare at his chest. "You know why."

I swallowed hard. "Enlighten me."

He leaned forward, lips brushing the very edge of my ear ever so softly. "Because I *want* to."

"But why?" I asked in a breath. "Why come to me at all if you can't have me? Why chase? You believe me to be your atma, but I reject that. I reject you. So why do you continue?"

Two fingers curved under my chin and lifted my face to meet his. I didn't want to look into his eyes. To stare at perfection so beautiful it hurt. The kind of beauty he had wasn't soft or kind. It was brutal. Honest. Cutting.

"Do you know what an atma is?" he asked me.

"A soulmate."

His full lips curved upward, and my heart stuttered. "Do you know what a soul is?"

"The concept that our true form is inside us somehow, but it isn't a physical being," I said, narrowing my eyes at him.

"Magic," he said simply. "Demons are beings made of magic. Once we were angels, but over time all magic corrupts. It slowly drives us to insanity. To darkness. Unless we find and bond with our atma." He brought his thumb down, sweeping it across my bottom lip. His pupils dilated at the movement, and a shudder ran through me. "I have waited thousands of years for you. I don't plan to wait another second. So if the only way I can see you right now is in your sleep, then I will. I'll take any time I can get, but one day you will be mine in every sense of the word."

He was staring at my lips too much. The tension was too thick. My throat felt full, and I swallowed hard, then looked away.

Just like last time, he let me. But he didn't move.

"That's a beautiful story, really, so touching," I said sarcastically. "There's only one problem with it. I'm not a demon."

"You weren't born one. That doesn't mean you aren't one." One of his hands wrapped around my forearm. The slight pressure of his fingers *burned* through me. My heart sped up.

"I stole the magic from one, that's not the same—"

"Actually," he said, "it is. The magic and the soul are the same. Your magic calls to me, just as mine

175

calls to you. Doesn't it, Atma?" His fingers on my arm loosened, sweeping up and over my shoulder, past my collarbone, to my neck.

"I told you not to call me that," I snapped at him, trying to step away. His fingers dipped inside the turtleneck I wore, even though it was a dream.

"Why does it bother you?" he asked, tilting his head.

"Because it's not my name."

"Liar," Ronan said. "You've never cared what people called you. Kenneth du Lac used the wrong name for two months before the summoning. You never corrected him once."

"Maybe I was scared."

"You? Scared?" He chuckled and leaned forward. "You were never scared. There's a reason the demon you called forth from the nether was one of rage. You called one that was well-met. She would have sensed your likeness and come to you willingly, except instead of crossing into the plane, you both collided. Aeshma was thousands of years old. One of the oldest, and she met her match in a sixteen-year-old child. Yet you want me to believe you were *scared*?" He laughed, but it wasn't kind or joyful. "You don't get scared. You get angry."

"Maybe it makes me angry, then," I said, heart beating faster. He was goading me, and I knew it, but didn't know how to stop.

"Why?" he said, taking another step forward. I mirrored him and took one back. His hand tightened around my throat, but not to crush it. The hold was possessive. Feral. "Is it because of your own prejudice?"

"Yes," I hissed.

He stared at me with black fire in his eyes. I wondered if my own did the same.

"No," he said. "You're still lying." Ronan leaned forward, and my breath slowed as my heart continued to speed up. I wondered if it would happen here. In my dreams. Would it bleed into the real world? Would I burn the cabin down?

"How would you know?"

"Because," he breathed, our faces only inches apart. "I can *feel* it."

His lips brushed against mine, and all rational thought came to a complete standstill.

It was soft, but not hesitant. The hold on my throat made me acutely aware of his every movement. Heat suffused me. Fire writhed. Conflicting emotions pulled taut within me, but there was one that won out above all.

Ronan pulled away, though it clearly took restraint for him to do so. He pressed his lips to the hollow of my ear and whispered. "Guilt. That's why we're here. That's why you hate being called my atma. That's why you'd see us both destroy each other." I tore myself away, working hard to control my breathing. Ronan took a step back and gave me a knowing look. "You picked this place as a reminder to yourself," he said, motioning to it. "And only you can tell yourself why."

His gaze looked through me, past my turtleneck and tight jeans. Past skin and muscle and bone. That thing he spoke of? It was there, and he stared it right in the face with unmasked longing and desire.

Then he gave me a cruel smirk and disappeared.

The dream faded into nothingness right before my eyes popped open.

The first stray rays of dawn peeked through the drapes. Gray, muted light replaced the heaviness of the cathedral.

I sat up, letting the sheet pool at my waist, and rubbed the sleep from my eyes. The dream sat on my chest like a brick weighing me down.

Because he was right.

Ronan was right.

Some people were driven by power and some by ambition and some by glory.

I was driven by guilt. Unending, all-consuming guilt.

Acknowledging it didn't change it. Talking about it didn't change it.

I made choices, and now I had to live with them.

Even if it destroyed me.

17

"Wouldn't it be more believable if I drove?"
Nathalie mused from the passenger seat beside me.
She had the window rolled down halfway, her long
nails tapping on the roof softly.

"You're what? Twenty-two? Do you even know
how to drive?" I asked skeptically.

Nathalie shrugged. "Can't be that hard. What's
that phrase you're so fond of? I'll just 'figure it out',"
she said with air quotes.

I snorted once. "Even if you managed to 'figure it
out' well enough that we didn't crash—no one would
buy that you apprehended me and then drove me to
the casino. I'm human, not a dumbass. I'd just jump
out."

It was her turn to snort. "And if someone sees us

with you driving me around? You think that's more believable?"

"No one is going to be looking for me in a car. I think it's safe to say you're fine," I said tepidly, as I turned onto a back road on the far side of town. It was still early morning, and few people were out on the streets. Mostly hookers and homeless. I really hoped my car wasn't stolen or jacked. I was going to need it to get back to Bree when this was all over.

If I could end it . . . I pushed the thought aside. Doubts wouldn't help me now.

We'd formulated a plan. All we had to do was play it out.

I pulled into a back lot that was deserted. Everything in it was broken down and trashed. The Honda with its cloaking device on would fit right in.

Quiet settled over us, followed by the screech of wind as I cut the engine.

"Are you sure you can do this?" I asked her quietly. "Because if you can't—"

"Piper, you said it yourself, I know how to lie and manipulate. I don't like doing it, but because of the family I grew up in, I learned from the best. I can get you in there. You're the one that's gotta hold on after that." Her brown eyes were serious. I saw that glint of amber again. It was only a sparkle for a fraction of a second, then it disappeared. "What?" she asked when I didn't respond.

"Nothing." I shook my head and reached for the door. "Let's do this."

The wind caught the door part way and flung it open. Cold hit me in the face. Crisp and clarifying. I hated the cold. At least it wasn't wet too.

With a dark look at the sky, as if tempting to open up and piss me off, I stepped out of the car and closed the door behind me. My windbreaker only helped so much as I walked around to the back and got slammed by gust after gust.

Windy City indeed, I thought, as I knelt down and felt under the grill for the device. My fingers skimmed the plastic edges, and I tapped the code, pressing each of them against it for just the right amount of time. The air rippled before the spell took effect. Spray paint appeared, and the paint began peeling. The tires deflated, and the glass shattered. The cushions ripped themselves on their own accord, and the steering wheel whined as the metal twisted and snapped.

I looked around, but no one was there to watch the transformation except me and Nathalie. My chest loosened a fraction as I got to my feet and held out a hand.

She blinked. "You just said driving you there wasn't an option."

"You're not driving," I replied. "You're holding the keys. I highly doubt they won't search me, and I don't want anyone finding them. That car is the only

way back to my sister. If this shitshow goes south . . ."
I didn't finish the sentence. Fear wouldn't help me
now. Neither would guilt.

Cold fingers brushed against mine as she took the
keys. "It's going to be fine," she said so serenely I
almost believed her . . . if I hadn't known by her own
admission that she was a capable liar. One half of her
pink mouth curved up and twisted in a smirk. "And if
it's not, I trust your ability to figure it out."

I groaned, the tension dissipating. "Are you ever
going to let that go?"

"Hmm," she said, touching the side of her mouth
like she was thinking. "Probably not." She shrugged,
turning on her heel.

"It's a viable plan."

"In so much as you can call it a plan."

I rolled my eyes, following after. I could disagree
until I was blue in the face, but neither of us were
yielding. Arguing wouldn't change that. All it would
do was draw unneeded attention to us.

I stepped up to her side, and we fell into an easy
rhythm, taking the back alleys through the streets until
we reached a more populated part of the city. While
supernaturals were more often than not creatures of
the night, humans still did most of their dealings
during the day. It was safer, especially when there was
no one to stop bad things from happening anymore.
Not since the government collapsed, and with it, all

support systems, including the police. Unless a human had to work with the supernatural directly, they were better off when most supes were sleeping and had strength in numbers. Or so the theory went. Realistically, numbers were a moot point when a werewolf or vampire could slaughter dozens in a minute flat. Human patrol existed to prevent that, or rather to deal with the aftermath when it did. Nothing brought those people back, though, and often the hunters working for patrol died at an early age. It wasn't an easy job when the cards were stacked in favor of the supe every time. That was half the reason we were doing this in the morning. Less competent bounty hunters that might try to steal me off of Nathalie. With most of the supes asleep, I felt confident she could probably fend off any humans without much of an issue.

"You should make the catch here. It's only twenty minutes from the casino."

We looked down the empty street. There was an L station not far, probably only three or four minutes if I jogged. Around the corner, a little pizza place that survived the Magic Wars because the owner's granddaughters were half-fae. A convenience store that wasn't so lucky sat across from it. The windows were shattered, and the store emptied of anything remotely edible long ago. Balconies lined the buildings five or six stories tall, which meant this was largely a residential section where more fortunate humans lived. The not-lucky ones got the street or were sold into slavery.

"So how do you want to do this?" Nathalie asked. "Do you just start running and I chase you, or what—"

I slapped a pair of handcuffs in her loose fingers and then punched her in the gut. The air left her lungs as she hunched over. Her watery eyes went wide with shock, then narrowed. "Seriously?" she hissed.

"Now I run," I said, then turned on my heel and took off down the street. The wind roared in my ears, and my heart rate picked up as I heard footsteps behind me. She was going to have a hard time catching me if I ran too far. I had a solid six inches more in height and twice as much muscle from doing this job for a decade.

I turned at the corner where the convenience store had been and jogged toward the park. A place filled with rusted and spray-painted assortments of playground equipment looked like the perfect place for this. Public enough, but not many people.

The footsteps behind me gained speed, and I slowed just a fraction to let her eat up ground. I crossed from the grass to the more cushioned rubber pavement and jumped over a plastic unicorn that rocked back and forth on a giant spring.

The breath hissed between her teeth, and a low muttering of words were only just reaching me as the monkey bars broke apart in front of me. Their metal hands reached, trying to bind my own. I turned and lifted an eyebrow at Nathalie, my jaw locked tight, as if to ask her, *really? Magic?*

She lifted her shoulders in the slightest shrug as if responding, *you wanted this to be believable, didn't you?*

I did, and I didn't.

It was not even twenty-four hours ago I'd accused her of being a spy, and now here we were, her playing bounty hunter to hand me over. If that wasn't ironic, I didn't know what was.

"You won't catch me," I said, taunting her.

"I already have." She grinned. I shot to the side, prepared to fend off the moving metal pipes reaching for me. Instead of circling my hands, though, they went for my feet. I jumped, trying to avoid their creeping grasp, but one I didn't see came around to hook my ankle. It snagged. I went down.

The bar tried to tighten, and I shook my leg, a real panic beginning to sink in.

This is Nathalie, I reminded myself. *She's lived with you for a week and saved your ass again and again.*

The cold metal wrapped around me, climbing my leg like a live vine.

I pulled my pistol and aimed it at her.

A small, not very rational part of me was tempted to shoot. She looked the part of a hunter, her face filled with impassioned arrogance as she stood over me. At seeing the gun pointed right between her eyes, her mask cracked, just a fraction.

She let me see her concern and silently seemed to ask me if I'd changed my mind.

My body went slack. I lowered the gun just enough to hold the ruse while letting her know to keep it up.

Another bar shot for my wrist, then froze. It quivered midair in front of me. Nathalie frowned. Then it began turning in on itself. The metal twisting and twining, retreating.

I could tell from the look on her face that wasn't supposed to happen.

She muttered again. The bar paused. Quivered. Then completely disintegrated. All of them did. Including the one around my ankle.

I gave her a not-amused look, and she flashed me one right back.

Before either of us could respond, a howl filled the air.

Then another.

And another.

Wolves the size of cars entered the park and were circling us in a second flat. Six of them, to be exact.

"Shit," I muttered, getting to my feet.

I turned my back on Nathalie, facing the very real threat. They snarled in my direction, massive jaws snapping in a pretty clear impersonation of what would happen to my skull if I made a wrong move.

"These friends of yours?" Nathalie asked from behind me.

"I'm not sure . . ."

The pack of six stopped, paused, and then the one directly in front of me shifted.

A naked man, well over six feet tall and built of muscle, towered over me.

I squinted past the sun in my eyes that backlit him. He had a strong brow, and straining muscles. "Recognize me?" he said, all arrogance.

It clicked.

"The alpha from the bar," I said.

He grinned. It wasn't nice. "Bingo."

I took a step back, and he took one forward. "You shot me in the head. Scrambled my brains. If it weren't for my omega mate that ran, I wouldn't know who I was looking for."

I took another step, and a hand brushed against my side—then locked around my other pistol. Nathalie stepped into me from behind and put the gun to my head. Cool metal pressed into my temple.

My heartbeat kicked up a notch, but I wasn't scared.

"Back off," she said to the alpha. "She's mine."

He looked over my shoulder and narrowed his eyes, then threw his head back and laughed. "You?"

he said. "Take it from me, little girl, you were never going to get her there, anyway. She didn't make a name for herself by being easily caught. I didn't know who I tangled with a week ago, but your boss burned you. I can see why you were so confident before, but now . . . we'll be collecting that bounty."

"How'd you find me?" I asked.

He held up his arm. Something was jutting out of it. I squinted.

"Vampire tooth," he said. "From the bar. Got yourself bitten and then tossed it aside. Had just enough blood that I got a witch to do me a tracking spell. Turns out you're not popular amongst their kind. She didn't even charge me."

"Fucking supes," I growled.

"Back at you, hunter."

My heart kicked up another notch as the wolves closed in.

There were six of them, five of which were in their wolf form. Assuming I could even fire off all six shots, there wasn't enough time. One or both of us would be dead by the end of the encounter, and the whole reason Nathalie was taking me was so I wouldn't be injured. I didn't know if the hit on me said dead or alive, but either way had consequences, especially if I let these blokes do it.

Judging by the malicious grin on the alpha's face, I'd be beat within a half inch of my life. Until I went demon on their ass. At which point my secret would be blown, and this entire plan would go up in flames.

"I said, back off," Nathalie snapped. The metal barrel pressed harder into my temple. "Come any closer and I'll shoot. He's only paying one mil if she's brought in *alive*."

She didn't know that. While Anders said a million, he never stated if the boss wanted me hot or cold. She was bluffing through her damn teeth.

I tried not to let it show on my face as I watched the alpha squeeze his fists.

"You shoot, and we're both out the money," he said, not correcting her.

That meant . . . double shit. If the order was to have me brought in hot, that was *not* good.

"I'm willing to take that over giving it to you," she said, her voice strong and sure.

"He's still willing to pay a quarter mil if I bring her in dead. I could just kill you both." He shrugged. The fact that he dropped the amount so much for dead versus alive had me worried.

Lucifer was a vindictive asshole.

A cold laugh made my spine snap straight.

It was coming from Nathalie.

"I'm a Le Fay. What makes you think you'd win this fight, pup?" she said, sounding utterly fearless, even if her own heartbeat was drowning out my own.

I had to give it to her. Girl had balls.

The alpha twisted his lips, seeming to consider it. Her words were good, but were they good enough? Probably depended on if they saw the monkey bars disintegrate or not.

"I'll split it with you," he said. "Fifty-fifty."

Nathalie laughed callously. "Nah, you'll jump me the second I put this down. I'm not stupid." She lifted her free hand and started wiggling her fingers.

The wind blew harder, and he paled.

Most witches couldn't do magic without speaking.

It was rare but not unheard of for some witches to do it with their hands alone, and when they could, it was usually considered a sign of substantial power.

If I weren't being held hostage with a gun to my head, I might have been contemplating that little tidbit about her a lot more. As it was, the wind was enough to make the alpha step back.

"I'll send the others away," he said, gritting his teeth. It was starting to sound like pleading, and that wasn't a good sign for an alpha that wanted to stay alpha long-term.

"What makes you think that would make me split it with you?" Nathalie said.

"You might be powerful, witch, but six wolves is still a lot for you. Human bodies don't heal as easily as wolves. You think you could take all six of us at the same time? One swipe of claws, and you'd be down and out. I care about my pack, though, and don't want to lose any wolves when I don't have to."

Nathalie seemed to consider that, and I couldn't offer her any aid, given this whole thing counted on people believing she was a bounty hunter.

Eventually, she said, "Send the wolves away and have them patrol the streets so we don't run into any problems. I want this job done. You come with me, and we split it sixty-forty, since I did do all the work."

I could tell the alpha wanted to argue, but another twirl of her fingertips and a mist of rain had him cutting his losses. He nodded once. "Deal." He extended his hand.

I couldn't see Nathalie, but I could sense the derisive look she was giving him. "Forgive me for not moving this pistol, or my hand, until the wolves are gone," she said tersely.

He inclined his head and then flashed a look toward his pack. The group stepped back slowly. When they were halfway across the park, they each turned tail and scattered.

Nathalie dropped her wiggling fingers to my shoulder and the wind and misty rain stopped. "Either walk ahead or walk parallel, but I'm not doing this with you at my back," she said. The alpha grunted and motioned toward the road that led to the casino. They both turned, and I figured she was eyeing him the same as he was her.

Her foot nudged the back of my calf. "Get moving," she snapped.

I shook my shoulder and her hand tightened, nails digging into me through my jacket and turtleneck shirt.

"We could knock her out," the alpha suggested. I sent him a scathing look and started walking.

"Let me guess, you'll carry her? Fat chance. I'd rather keep her gun on you, and we go with her awake."

The alpha lifted both hands in mock surrender. "I'm just saying, it would solve a lot of our problems."

Nathalie didn't deign to give him a response, and neither did I.

The city was quiet as we made our way toward the casino in strained silence. My muscles were so contracted that I half expected to get a cramp. True to the werewolf's word, we made it to the back door without him trying anything. I sensed Nathalie tense at my back.

"Open it," Nathalie said.

My lips tightened in a grimace as I reached for the metal handle. The door squealed like a dying pig. The hall light flickered on and off. It wasn't the bustling place it usually was when I came in for my gigs. The door at the end wasn't in a constant rotation, instead it was closed and quiet. We approached the door on the right. My heartbeat kicked up again, and I took a breath through my nose and released it slowly, trying to calm my own nerves.

"Knock," she commanded.

I lifted my hand, unsure who would answer with Ronny dead.

My worry doubled down when it opened, and it was Anders' watery blue eyes that stared at me. His expression softened, then hardened. He stepped back, opening the door wide.

I'd never been on this side of the door.

Never seen much of it beyond Ronny's barreled chest.

I had to say, I was disappointed by the metal table and chairs. The walls were a pristine white. An elevator at the back. A single hook hung from the ceiling, one that I suspected Ronny had used to beat the shit out of people before they went wherever came next—probably through the elevator.

"I'm surprised," Anders said, motioning to the table. "I was so sure you'd never let anyone bring you in alive."

"Sorry to disappoint," I spat. Anders snapped his fingers and the elevator doors opened. Two men stepped out, both of them larger than the alpha escorting me.

"Grab her," he sighed. They moved faster than any humans, and before I could turn my gun on him, I was wrenched away from Nathalie and my arms pulled taut behind my back. One held me up, hand fisted in my hair. The other disarmed me, then patted me down, thankfully in a clinical manner instead of trying to cop a feel.

While they were busy, Anders invited Nathalie and the alpha douche to take a seat across at the table. On it, a single file sat next to an ashtray. Anders pulled out a cigarette and snapped his fingers again, this time with the other hand. A tiny spark lit. He touched the end of the cigarette to it. Smoke wafted off as he took a long drag before sitting down. He kicked his leg out, and I saw it had a cast on it. It was the same foot I'd shot.

"You two must be quite the team to catch this one and bring her in alive. She was our best hunter for years," Anders said, not touching the file. Dark circles lined his eyes. He looked tired. I imagine Lucifer had him here until someone brought me in.

"We're not a team," Nathalie said. "He just tried to steal my bounty."

"Oh?" Anders said. The guy patting me down fished my spare knife out of my boot and then gave the other one a grunt I had to assume meant I was all clear.

"She shot me a week ago. I had a bone to pick, but someone beat me to it." The alpha shrugged, not at all reproachful.

"Tell me, how'd you do it? I've had the rare pleasure of seeing her in action, and I gotta say, you don't look like you have much in you." He appraised her, and not in a creepy way, but like he was looking at another potential hunter.

"A good magician never reveals their secrets," Nathalie said with a grin and a wiggle of her fingers. A wind that didn't belong rustled the file, scattering some of the papers about.

"Fair enough," Anders said and shrugged. "I figured it must be quite the story how someone she'd kidnapped a week ago was now turning her in." He flicked the end of his cigarette, and ash dropped to the tray.

Nathalie's eyes widened almost imperceptibly. Anders' expression didn't change, and I cursed internally. He knew. I don't know how, but he did.

Anders always knew. There was a reason he'd had his job as long as he did, and it sure as shit wasn't because he was human.

"I gained her trust," Nathalie said, backtracking. "I played the part of hostage and then convinced her I wanted to team up. Then I waited until her guard was down."

"Hmm," Anders hummed. "Bounty wasn't on her when she kidnapped you."

"No, it wasn't," Nathalie agreed. "But by the time I wasn't a hostage anymore, it was. I decided to bide my time and wait for an opportunity."

Anders flicked his cigarette again. His expression hadn't changed once.

The elevator dinged, though no one had pressed the button.

I looked down at the paper in front of me right then. I'd assumed it had been on me. I was the target, after all.

Or so I thought.

The picture that stared back at me was Nathalie.

"Unfortunately for you, Ms. Le Fay, you're just as guilty. Piper Fallon might have been hired to kill you and your coven, but you summoned the demon to begin with."

The doors opened, and though I'd never seen him in my life, I knew without a shadow of doubt that the man I was staring at was the devil himself.

Lucifer was here.

1 8

He smiled with the light of a thousand suns.

The Morningstar, they called him.

I could see it. His white blond hair was worn short and spiky in a modern fashion, but there was no mistaking the glow that came from it. His golden eyes swirled with mercurial delight. A cruel grin crossed his perfect lips. Like Ronan, he dressed in a fine designer suit. Unlike him, his was white, whereas Ronan wore black, at least the times I'd seen him.

"Piper Fallon," he said in a voice like velvet. He could make humans weep just from the sound of it. I was glad he didn't now. "And Nathalie Le Fay." He turned that blinding smile on her. Nathalie jumped to her feet, knocking the chair over in the process.

"Boss," I said the word sarcastically.

That voluptuous smile faded. The mirth in his

expression dimmed as the rage that he was equally known for started to surface.

"Ex," he snapped. "You betrayed me."

"You were a job," I said. "Grow the fuck up. It's not like I was contractually bound. You hired me to hunt down the people that pissed you off, and this time I chose to use them for my own benefit."

The room went silent as everyone held their breath. Those golden eyes focused on me.

"Yes," he purred. "I hired you to bring me the people who lied to me. Stole from me. Imagine," he said, striding forward and reaching up to run his fingers down my cheek, "what I do to people who betray me."

I spat at him. The wet glob hit him right in the face.

His ire rose. Power gathered in the air around us. The tattoos that peeked out at the neckline and cuffs of his suit flared to life, glowing white hot.

A cold hand wrapped around my throat.

It felt like marble, smooth and strong.

He started to close his fingers, cutting off the air in my windpipe.

Panic flared inside me, and I had to fight my heartbeat to slow.

It wasn't time yet.

Lucifer leaned in, and I got the impression he was going to tear me a new one. Then he paused.

His rage evaporated like alcohol in open air. His fingers loosened, taking a different hold. A possessive one.

He leaned in, his nose trailing along my jaw, inhaling deeply.

Then he purred.

Goosebumps pebbled my skin.

"Uh, boss?" the man holding my arms behind my back said.

Lucifer lifted his head and stared at the guard. There was death in his eyes when he let out a growl. "Why are you questioning me?"

"I, uh," the man fumbled. I wanted to roll my eyes. While big and clearly strong, they weren't the brightest. At least this one wasn't.

"You don't have a reason?" Lucifer asked, voice clipped.

"Well, I—"

"You don't have a reason," Lucifer repeated, not a question.

"I don't have a reason," the guard repeated slowly. Fear crept into his voice. Lucifer tsked.

"Perhaps you shouldn't speak unless spoken to, then? Hm?" he said, his eyes glowing. "Cut out your tongue."

The hands gripping me turned sweaty.

"Sir?"

That ire inside him burned once more. "I said, Cut. Out. Your. Tongue."

I didn't look, but the hands that were holding mine behind my back released me. I kept the shock from my face as the sounds of whimpers and pain started. I tried not to react as wordless cries fell on deaf ears. Blood dripped to the ground. A pool began forming around my left boot.

I heard his knees hit the cement floor and couldn't stop my nose from wrinkling as his hand fell to the side. Holding the bleeding stump of his tongue.

"Does anyone else feel like questioning me?" Lucifer asked, looking around the room. "No?" Everyone save me shook their head. "How about you, Piper? Feeling mouthy?" he said, giving me an amused grin as he pulled the handkerchief from his suit pocket and wiped the spit off his face.

"No."

"Good," he beamed, flashing me that radiant smile. "Because I'm sure we can find much better uses for that mouth of yours if you feel like running it again."

Heat blossomed in his gaze, and my stomach turned.

First Ronan, now Lucifer.

Both were vile creatures from Hell. Except where Ronan's intensity made my heart beat wildly, Lucifer just made my skin crawl. He was a level of crazy that the rumors didn't do justice.

"You," he said, turning to the alpha. The man swallowed hard and pointed at himself as if in question. Lucifer rolled his eyes. "Yes, you. I find myself in need of another guard. Congratulations. You're hired."

"But I—" the alpha started.

"But you *what?*" Lucifer said, his voice going quiet as a hiss.

"I need clothes," the man finished. While it wasn't all that uncommon to see naked people in New Chicago because of the large shifter population, most at least had the common decency to cover it.

"Anders, get the man some clothes. New guard, grab her," he pointed at Nathalie.

She backed away, lifting her hand. Winds started to whip again, the careful calm she'd emulated before now gone.

The alpha looked between her and Lucifer.

The demon groaned. "Do I have to do everything myself?" he asked to no one in particular. I was starting to wonder if he was talking to a voice in his head.

Lucifer gave Nathalie a sharp glare, his eyes glowing once more. "Stop scaring him with the show. Put your hands behind your back."

The wind stopped at once. Nathalie's hand

dropped, and she turned, presenting her wrists with a dazed look.

"You. Other guard," Lucifer said to the one at my side. He'd smartly kept his mouth shut and not moved. "Hold her securely. Or do you need to chop your hands off because they're useless?"

"No, sir." The guard stepped behind me and grabbed my wrists firmly.

"Finally! Someone that understands how to take orders," Lucifer said, throwing his hands up. "Anders, get this mess cleaned up. And you"—he turned to me once more, his cold fingers wrapping around my throat—"I was going to kill you. I debated having you rip yourself apart, a very apt punishment for betrayal, is it not?"

I pressed my lips together, trying to keep myself from saying anything that might get *my* tongue ripped out. He smirked, his hand loosening. "But your smell . . . it's familiar. Divine. You're not going anywhere until I figure out why you smell like my atma."

Shock ran through me.

This couldn't be happening.

I couldn't be two demons' atma.

I couldn't even be one.

Yet, here was another demon, claiming I was their soulmate. It appeared that somewhere along the way, the universe just decided to fuck me in every way possible.

Lucifer smiled coldly. "I like you better this way. Now go to sleep. I don't need you overpowering anyone on the way."

"The way to where?" I asked, fighting against the instant urge to sleep. I stifled a yawn.

"Sleep," Lucifer commanded again. Darkness was falling as the last of his words reached me. "You'll see when we get there."

And then it was silence.

———

"PIPER." My name was whispered from across the void. Deep. Husky. Full of want and desire and some-thing else. Something that made me shiver.

"Ronan?" I questioned. Shadows swirled in front of me, forming the demon. Instead of a suit, he came to me in sweats that hung low on his hips. His skin was slick with sweat, making the contours of his shirt-less abdomen glisten. His brands pulsed with dark power. Markings that I didn't truly understand hugged both sides of his abs and ran across his broad chest. Both arms were covered from wrist to shoulder, creeping up the thick column of his neck.

I swallowed. My mouth felt dry.

"It's early," he mused. "You usually sleep at night like the humans, unless . . ." His voice trailed, and dark fire flashed in his eyes. "Did you use your power? I didn't feel it."

He could feel it?

That was possible?

I grimaced. "Is that a side effect of the blood-exchange as well?"

"No," he said. "It's a side effect of being a demon of great power. I can feel the fluctuations in your world easily because so little magic exists here compared to my own." Ronan took a step closer. "But you didn't answer my question," he said softly. "Did. You. Use. Your. Power?" He enunciated every word softly, but it was not kind.

I glared at him, unamused by his alphaholeness. I'd grown up among shifters and vampires. Incubi. Warlocks. Fae. They were all the same in that. He didn't scare me.

"What's it matter if I did?" I said, choosing to not answer his question and instead see if I could get more information out of him. Ronan's nostrils flared. He didn't like my tone. Well, I didn't like his.

"If you did, and I didn't feel it, that means you're in trouble. While you can run from me all you like, I don't want others butting into my game. You're *mine*. Mine to chase. Mine to claim. Mine to protect."

"I don't need your protection," I said.

"But you need me to chase?" he asked darkly,

amusement flitted through his features. "To claim?"
My skin flushed.

"That is *not* what I meant."

Ronan snorted once. It was an odd thing to see. A
demon acting so human, especially after watching
Lucifer. He was anything but.

Ronan took a step back, letting me breathe. He
circled me slowly, examining me from all angles. "I
know you don't need my protection. Perhaps what I
feel is closer to possessiveness. After so long of
searching and failing so far . . . I can't let you slip
through my grasp. I'll give you time. You'll find that
I'm a patient man, but Piper . . ." He paused in front
of me and leaned in. Eyes like the winter skies pulled
me into their depths. "I always get what I want."

"You're not a man," I said.

He grinned savagely. "You're right, I'm not. I'm so
much worse." He brushed a fingertip over my clothed
forearm. "And so much better."

I snorted, rolling my eyes. "That's what they all
say."

He paused, frowning. "Who is this 'they'?"

I couldn't tell if this was a moment where his
knowledge of my world and our euphemisms fell
short, or if it was jealousy. Primal. Lethal.

If I had to guess, I'd say it was probably both.

I stepped back, and his hand dropped from me.
This conversation was coming dangerously close to

flirting, and I didn't flirt. Not with human men. Not with supernatural men. And certainly, not with demons.

"Is it possible for someone to have more than one atma?" I asked, changing the subject. Ronan narrowed his eyes.

"Why do you ask?"

"Why do you? We keep doing this, going around and around in circles. I need answers. Either you can give them to me, or I can find someone else." I crossed my arms over my chest and lifted an eyebrow. "So which will it be?"

Ronan didn't seem to like this exchange of power. Unfortunately for him, I didn't give a shit.

"No," he said after a moment. "There's only ever one atma, and if you lose her"—he snapped his fingers—"that's it. No second chances. The madness will eat you alive as your power grows until you self-destruct. Now, why are you asking me this?"

I lifted one shoulder in a disinterested fashion, preparing to bait him. If Nathalie couldn't go find him now that I'd been taken, this was my next best shot—and the backup plan to the first one. "Call it curiosity. I met another demon. He also claimed I'm his atma."

Ronan froze. Black fire actually erupted at his hands, and it took all my willpower to not step back as its dark heat bathed my face.

"He's lying."

I shrugged again. "He said I smelled like his atma. I don't know how specific these things are. Maybe you're lying. Maybe neither of you are, and the universe just thought it would be funny. Either way, I'm not bonding to either of you fuckers."

The fire winked out, and Ronan took a couple of ragged breaths.

"Are you playing me, Piper?"

I froze. "What?"

"Are you trying to make me—what's the word— jealous? Trying to incite my wrath? You won't accept my bond, yet your body begs so sweetly . . ." His eyes trailed down my form as if he could see and feel it begging. "I want more than your body, though. I want your mind. I want your heart. I want your fucking soul." He stepped toward me. "It's mine, Piper. I know that. You know that, even though you're fighting it. No one else gets a cut. I *do not share.* So are you playing me? Because every time I've been near you, your magic comes out to play. Yet, you say another demon calls you his atma. Did your magic respond then? Did *you?*"

He was leaning close, and the scent of dark magic, midnight shadows, and a musk that I couldn't place enveloped me.

Time slowed as we stared at each other.

And then he said in that voice of dark desire, "It didn't, did it?"

"My magic lashing out isn't a sign of some great bond or love or whatever you want to call it. You've said yourself, it's rage. Pure, unequivocal rage. Maybe you should be asking yourself why it didn't respond to him?" I said softly, steel edging my tone.

I could tell he did not like that answer.

"I suppose it doesn't matter. Either way, you've said what I needed to know. You're with another demon, and you're asleep when you shouldn't be, which means you're in grave danger." Ronan stepped away, his gaze troubled. I had a feeling there was something he'd figured out that he wasn't saying.

"Where are you going?" I asked as he stalked away into the void.

Ronan paused and looked over his shoulder, dark promise in his eyes. "Don't enter a blood-exchange with him."

I blinked. That wasn't what I expected him to say. "Why?" I prompted.

"It could kill you."

19

RONAN

SHE WAS PLAYING WITH FIRE.

While she'd revealed more than she realized, she was also holding back. Hiding something. I knew it as surely as I knew she was my atma.

The desire to know what it was ate at me like a blood-sucking parasite buried beneath the skin. My lips tightened into a thin line. I sat up, dropping the six-hundred-pound bar I'd been bench pressing. I felt her sleeping.

She may have detested me, but her mind always sought my own during that time. I simply entered her dreams and allowed it. My atma might be cold, and even cruel in her own way, but she was also mine.

And she needed me. Not that she seemed to realize it.

That stubborn woman would drink poison before

asking for my help. That quality almost made me admire her more—if she weren't so willfully blind to her own needs.

I stood up and walked out of the home gym. The sounds of the city were more muted from here, but not gone entirely. I listened to them as I padded silently to the bathroom for a shower.

I flipped the water to cold, and then stepped in.

It helped cool my blood and urges where Piper was concerned.

Damned woman made me want to strangle her and fuck her in equal measure in the short time I'd been here.

Mentally, I reached out to my errand boy. My mind touched his, only the briefest of connections so I could tell him, "Get in touch with your friend. I need to know where Piper is."

"I'll try."

"If you can't reach her, then get me a location on Lucifer. It's past time I paid him a visit."

With that, I retreated from the boy's mind and turned all thoughts to Piper. Despite the cold water running down my body, my cock hardened at the memory of her ocean blue eyes, the way they narrowed at me in rage. Her full lips pursed in indignation. Her cheeks flushed with anger.

Yes, she hated me. I'd come to grips with that. Some might even say I liked it. Embraced it.

I was an old demon. One from an era long gone. I'd waited so long for her that I actually enjoyed this game we were playing. I enjoyed her hate. Her rage.

Because her surrender when she gave it up would be all the sweeter.

My eyes opened before I could ask him anything further. The void disappeared, replaced by low ambient lighting. I turned my head to see a man's back. He faced the other way, looking out a window that spanned the length of the wall, floor to ceiling. He wore white, and his hands clasped behind his back.

Lucifer.

I blinked twice, trying to clear the sleep from my eyes, then I swallowed hard. My throat was dry. *How long had I been asleep?*

"There's water on the end table. Drink it." His lilting voice washed over me. It poked and prodded, looking for my weak spots. I resisted it through sheer force of will, but I sat up all the same. My back was sore, and my head scrambled. Everything was foggy, as if my mind had been filled with cotton.

I took a sweeping glance of the space and found we were alone in a darkened room. Music played softly, only sounds without words. A grand piano sat untouched at the other side of the room. Its black wood polished and shining beneath the spotlights. I was seated on a long white modern couch. Two matching chairs sat at either end, facing inward. The couch faced the window, but from this vantage point I couldn't see much.

I reached for the water. The glass was cool against my fingers. I had to resist pressing it against my forehead and instead swallowed it down, hoping it wasn't poisoned or drugged. It wasn't like I had many other options. Ronan would either find me, or he wouldn't.

"How are you feeling?" Lucifer asked, still facing away from me. I found it odd given the madness I'd seen. He didn't strike me as the type of person to give a shit about others.

"I've been worse," I said, testing my voice. It was hoarse, but the water had helped. "Where am I?" I asked, setting the glass back down.

"We're still in New Chicago," Lucifer answered.

I leaned forward, testing my muscles. They felt fine, if not a bit sore. I stood up and walked toward the window. My breath caught in my chest.

"The Underworld?" I said. Below us, stands rose

up on all sides. A sandpit sat in the middle of the arena. The walls were stained reddish-brown with blood. More of the substance covered the arena, and I chose not to look too closely at the two people fighting in it.

"You recognize it?"

"There's only one place in New Chicago that allows pit fights," I said instead of answering. "Or I suppose I should say, only one place you allow. All others, human or not, you shut down before they got going. Must make for good business when yours is the only one around."

In truth, I'd managed to sneak in here twice. Both times for targets. The Underworld was a place that only supes could go. Within its borders, humans were sold and killed with no consequences, and no one bothered to stop it. I didn't exactly make a point to visit when I identified as human.

"You must not come here often, or I'd have found you long before now," Lucifer said, ignoring the rest of my statement. My muscles locked up.

"I worked for you for three years, and you never noticed me," I replied.

His perfect lips curled up on one side as he finally looked at me. Slow. His gaze roaming. Undressing. My hand instinctively went for my gun. But my holster was gone, along with any weapons I might have had. I closed my fist and squeezed, never having felt so powerless.

"You're wrong. I noticed, but I thought you were human. Your kill count was higher than any hunter, supernatural or not. I should have looked closer. I'll admit that. My arrogance blinded me from thinking there might be more to you."

There was a lot of what he had said that was fucked up, but the thing my brain focused on was *I thought you were human.*

"I am human," I said, repeating that tired line.

Lucifer turned away from the match entirely and took a step toward me. Mirth danced in his expression again. Along with something else. "You expect me to believe that?" he asked, lifting both brows. "I questioned Anders. He claims the same. If it weren't for my compulsion being infallible, I'd have thought he was lying," Lucifer said. He took a step toward me. I stood my ground, glaring up at him. The demon reached for me, and I slapped his hand away.

A hint of his ire, his fury, bled into his expression.

Lucifer's eyes glowed, but then as fast as the change had happened, it halted.

He smiled, and it was more unsettling than his anger.

"I scent your fear and your anger. It's an intoxicating combination."

My stomach turned in disgust, reminding me to

not be fooled by his pretty face. It was a mask for a monster. "Why am I here?"

"In the Underworld?" He motioned outward. "Because you betrayed me. Or do you mean here? With me?" My silence said more than words. His smile widened. "Because you smell like my atma, and I want to know *why*."

"I don't know why," I said.

Lucifer reached for me, and this time when I tried to shake him off, he didn't allow it. His arm encircled my waist and his hand gripped my hip. Nails dug into my flesh as he turned us both away from the window and led me toward the couch. "Actually, I think you do. You just might not realize it yet."

A foot away from the couch, Lucifer pushed me. I went willingly and whirled around, expecting the worst. But he didn't sit next to me or come down on top of me. He stepped away and began pacing while rubbing his palms together.

"The witch I interrogated that night said it was a male demon that crossed over," he started. I squinted up at him. He paused and looked at me expectantly, waiting for an answer.

"It was," I said slowly. He nodded.

"So she must have crossed over before then," he said. "Maybe she sought you out. Have you had contact with any other demons?" His eyes glowed, and I felt a power I'd never known pressing against me. It was seeking. Searching. He wanted the truth.

I was choking on it.

"Yes," I said, unable to stop myself.

His smile widened, golden eyes blazing more than before. "When?"

"A decade ago."

The words came from lips, though I fought them. Fought and failed.

I hated it.

His nose crinkled. I couldn't tell if he disliked my answer or if he was confused by it.

"But you smell like her now," he said, then returned pacing. The crowd from the arena roared. If I had to guess, someone had died. Lucifer didn't look up. It was beneath his interest when the prospect of his atma was within his reach. Or so he thought.

I shrugged. "I don't know what to tell you." My heartbeat was picking up the more power he funneled into me.

"How did you meet her? Tell me everything."

I shuddered under the growing pressure. Words forced themselves up my throat and past my lips. "There was a summoning," I said. "A different coven than this one. I was the sacrifice. Or I was supposed to be."

"What happened?" he asked, dark emotion entering his voice. He came to kneel in front of me.

"We tore a rift between the worlds and put out a call. The demon that answered—" I tried to fight it. To halt the words. To not spill my secrets at his feet. Lucifer's eyes narrowed, and he placed his hands on either side of my face. Power slammed into me. My heartbeat thrummed, then raced. Adrenaline was flooding my system. I didn't have long. His eyes shined so bright I had to close my own against the glare.

"Who answered?" he asked, his tenor ten times deeper than it had been before. All other sound was muted outside his voice, and my heartbeat raced toward that dreadful stop.

"Aeshma," I bit out. "She came to me. To bargain."

"What did you ask for?"

Water built behind my eyelids and a single tear dripped down my cheek in the face of such immense strength. "Power," I admitted. Shame filled me.

"Why?" he demanded. "Anders said you hate magic."

"I didn't always." My voice trembled. "I was five when the president was killed on TV. Magic became known when I was just a child, and I wanted it more than *anything*. For years, I searched for a way."

"Then you found one," he surmised. "You joined the circle to call her for the promise of power." I sensed something in his voice. Like something had occurred to him that hadn't before. "She gave it to you?" he asked.

Faster. Faster. Faster.

I had moments at most.

"Yes," I said.

Lucifer released me. The power that had been flooding my system drained away. I opened my eyes.

He leaned away, assessing me carefully.

"Then that's why you smell like her. You carry a piece of her in you. I'm going to use that to find her."

In that moment, two things hit me, and they were absolutely vital to my survival.

The first was that I was not his atma. Aeshma was.

The second was that I lied. Somehow.

Aeshma didn't give me this power. I took it.

And now Aeshma was dead.

LUCIFER EASED BACK, giving me space. My heartbeat slowed. Adrenaline drained away. He sat back on his haunches.

"You're a curious creature, Piper Fallon," he said. "I'm tempted to taste you. Can you imagine her ire at me for defiling her servant?" he said softly. He reached out, letting his fingers trail up my jaw. His hand went behind my head and fisted in my hair. "It might be enough to bring her to me. I wouldn't even have to look." He licked his lips. Desire that wasn't my own thickened the air. "Or I could just have you in other ways. Your scent alone is enough to get me off."

"You would do that? Even when you have an atma?" I said. I hoped that reminding him of that might keep him at bay. It's not like his atma would ever show. But if she were his soulmate, wouldn't he feel something toward her?

"Aeshma rejected me. If she's on this plane, that means she must have realized her own folly. She might be my atma and the center of my desire, but that doesn't mean she's the only one. You have some of her blood. You'd be more durable than the others. A fun toy to break . . ." He pulled me toward him, and I couldn't resist. Our foreheads touched and his eyes closed, inhaling deeply. "You were her first blood servant, and she's only been here ten years. She would feel a connection to you. Your pain . . . it would incite her."

What little my heart had eased was starting to rise once more. My blood pulsed through my veins, pounding in my ears.

He was wrong. I didn't have any of Aeshma's blood. She never gave me any.

Would I still taste like her? Or would he be able to tell?

His lips slanted toward mine. Their velvety softness briefly brushed over my own, eliciting a groan from him.

A knock came at the door.

Lucifer paused.

"What?" he demanded, pulling back. The door opened, but he didn't look away from my lips.

"Sir, the witch's fight is about to begin." I couldn't

place the voice beyond it being male, and that told me very little about who they were.

Lucifer sighed. "Very well, we'll be down in a moment."

The door closed once more. Lucifer's tongue traced the bottom of his teeth, as if he considered going for another taste before the fight. His eyes twinkled with cruel amusement as he stood up, dragging me with him by his hold on my hair.

"Come along," he said, dropping his hold to take my hand. I glowered at it. "Take my hand," he bit out, his eyes glowing for a brief second. I gave in to the power and took his hand in mine, letting him pull me along.

Outside the room it was dark. The hallways were lit by fluorescent, unappealing light. They had concrete floors that were cracked in places. Reddish-brown stains pooled every few feet. I knew without asking it was from blood. How many people could bleed in a hallway and for what reason wasn't that far beyond my imagination.

We continued onward, turning corners before heading down a set of stairs. The sounds of the crowd grew as we stepped out of an opening. To our left, a set of stairs went all the way down to the sand-pit, not ten feet from us. To the right, a couple of larger steps ascended to a dais of sorts, where a gaudy throne sat.

Lucifer went for the throne, tugging me along behind him.

The crowd quieted.

Lucifer took his seat, releasing my hand. I stood there, crossing my arms over my chest. "I take it you expect me to stand here?"

"Of course not," he said, still smiling. "Would you rather sit at my feet like a pet, or sit on my lap like a whore?"

My lips parted, but I bit back the snarky reply where I'd tell him to go fuck himself. That would only make my situation worse.

"Feet," I said, after a suspended second.

"Very well," he grinned. I turned to kneel, facing the pit, but two cold hands grabbed my waist. He pulled me back onto his lap. My ass positioned over his half-hard cock.

"You just said—"

"I asked which you'd prefer, I didn't say you actually had a choice," he hummed, wrapping a strong arm around my middle. He pulled me flush against his chest. His free hand knotted in my hair, pulling it hard. My neck craned back and to the side, manipulated at his whim. Cool lips brushed up the column of my throat.

"Begin," he announced.

The crowd went wild now that the uncrowned King of New Chicago was here. In the sandpit, two doors on either side of it opened. On one side, a tall, lean woman strode forward. She wore black leather pants and knee-high boots. Her small breasts were strapped to her chest in some kind of black halter top. Golden tattoos lined her right arm, standing stark against her dark brown skin. She had long black hair pulled back into a sleek, high ponytail, showing off her pointed ears. Fae.

She lifted her chin to the crowd, and they began chanting, "Dara! Dara! Dara!"

On the other side of the ring, a much smaller, much dirtier, Nathalie stumbled out. Her brown hair was pulled back harshly in a bun. Her eyes were sharp, and her nose red from rubbing it. She was dressed the same as I'd last seen her, and overall, none the worse for wear.

"Have I mentioned how delicious you smell?" Lucifer said, tugging at my hair as if he could sense my attention waning. My eyes cut sideways and narrowed, though he couldn't see them.

"A time or two," I replied caustically. His length hardened beneath me.

The fae woman pulled a whip from her side and cracked it once.

Blue lightning arced down it.

Nathalie paled, but she stood straight and didn't cower.

Lips grazed my skin, making me freeze. I couldn't

hold back the growl, and Lucifer purred, content as a fucking cat to play with his food.

"You don't like my touch?" he asked.

"I'm not surprised you get off on forcing women. Only repulsive men that can't get laid otherwise do that."

Lucifer stilled. "You think I can't find willing participants?"

I turned my chin to look at him, and the grip in my hair eased. "Is it willing if you order them to?"

His golden eyes bore into mine. Neither of us were watching the match below, and I had a feeling it would be short. I needed to find a way to stop it and get out.

"I could make you beg for it."

"That only proves my point."

"I could do it without ordering you," he said, his tone sharpening.

"Could you do it without magic?" I said, braver than I felt.

His icy features hardened, and I let my lips curl up on one side.

"Of course."

"Hmm," I hummed, debating how far I could go before I incited his wrath. In the pit, the fae woman lunged, and Nathalie dove to the side, barely getting out of the way of the whip as it cracked. A bolt of lightning struck the side of the ring, and a fissure formed in the concrete siding. "I thought you were going to kill her." Nodding toward the pit.

"The Le Fay girl?"

"Were you planning to kill the other one too?"

"At first, yes," he said, leaning back to watch them once more. My pulse slowed a small fraction. We were treading dangerously close. "Dara Lightseeker can control lightning, though. Useful skill. Rare. I made her a deal instead. She's now my top pit fighter."

"And Nathalie?" I asked.

"Bait, but if she survives this fight, she'll be sold to the highest bidder. I find slavery is worse than death in most cases. Before she just tried to summon a demon, and that warranted death. Then she helped you." He paused as Dara closed in on Nathalie. Her whip wrapped around the witch's ankle, tripping her. Nathalie fell face-first into the sand. "I can't have that. It sets a poor example to simply kill her. You two have thrown off the order of things, but in selling her, and breaking you—I show my subjects what will become of them if they upset me."

I swallowed and looked at the ceiling. High above us, cement and metal pipes lined the top of the arena. Spotlights dangled from the pipes to illuminate the pit. I had no idea how long had passed since he'd knocked me out. It could have been hours or days. Underneath the ground, though, there was no way to tell. Fortunately, not all of the Underworld was actually underground. I just needed to get free and find my way out. Well, that and find a way to stop the fight.

At the rate it was going, Nathalie didn't have long before the fae killed her. I wouldn't be far behind her once Lucifer's game came to an end. He'd either take a bite and would then learn his atma was dead, or he'd rape me first, then take a bite.

I was supposed to wait for Ronan and let him take on Lucifer while Nathalie and I got away. That was the plan.

As the fae woman picked Nathalie up with one hand and slammed her against the wall, I knew in my bones that this was it.

I may not know her well, but she'd stuck her neck out for me again and again. And this fae was going to slaughter her if I did nothing.

But could I? That was a stupid question to ask myself. My racing heart said I very much could. Would I? That was a better question. A smarter one.

To change her fate would change my own. Lucifer and every other person here would see the truth of what I was.

Playing human after this wouldn't be possible.

But being dead was worse.

Right as I shifted my weight, resigned in my decision, Dara struck.

Lightning arced from one hand straight into Nat's chest.

She screamed, and blue light shone beneath her pale skin.

"No!" I shouted. Our eyes met.

Unbearable pain filled her expression as lightning coursed through her body.

I waited for her to lose consciousness. I waited for the pain to become too much. I waited for her skin to char and wither.

I waited for her to die.

It seemed that I was not the only one surprised when that didn't happen.

A second suspended in time. The look of pain changed over the length of it, and her eyes never looked away from me as they started to glow. A pure, brilliant gold.

She pressed her lips together, swallowing down the last of her screams, and I knew then that something was coming.

Nathalie reached for the hand holding her pinned, and the fae woman faltered. Her pale fingers wrapped around that darker wrist. Dara's strength waned, and Nathalie used that moment to strike. She canted forward and grabbed for Dara's face with her other hand. The fae stepped back, but Nathalie didn't stop. She didn't pause.

Her skin was glowing as she pressed her lips to Dara's.

The crowd stopped chanting.

Everything went quiet.

Then the fae exploded in a shower of ash and dust.

22

If I hadn't been dealing with all flavors of supes most of my life, my jaw might have dropped open. I knew she was weird and had strange magic, but I wasn't expecting that.

Judging by the slack grip around my waist and the silent arena—neither was anyone else.

Except Nathalie.

She held her chin high amid the plume of dust that was all that remained of Dara.

"Well, well, well," Lucifer murmured. He stood up, and I slid from his lap, disregarded at least for the moment. "What have we here?"

Nathalie didn't cower under his stare. She straightened her spine and fisted her hands at her sides.

"I asked you a question," Lucifer said, speaking

louder for her less advanced senses. The amusement dropping from his tone. "What are you?"

"A witch," she said, keeping her voice steady. She was thirty feet away, and yet I heard her as clearly as if she were next to me. I could only assume Lucifer did as well. "A gray witch."

He sneered coldly, disbelieving. "Try again," he said, his eyes glowing.

Nathalie grit her teeth, but it only took a second for the truth to force its way past her lips. "I don't know."

Lucifer frowned. That wasn't the answer he was suspecting.

"Come here," he commanded.

Nathalie's feet moved robotically as she crossed the sandy pit and came to stop at the bottom of the stairs. While she was strong, I could see my own panic mirrored in her face.

"Give me your wrist."

Nathalie lifted her hand. Her fingers shook, whether from trying to fight the compulsion or from fear, I wasn't sure.

Lucifer grabbed it, pulling it to his face. He inhaled deeply.

His fangs extended.

His eyes glowed brighter than before.

Then he bit her. Nathalie shuddered in revulsion as he took a single, long pull and then released her wrist. Blood smudged his mouth and her skin. She pulled her arm back to her chest, glaring defiantly at him. Lucifer tilted his head back, closing his eyes. A smile formed at the corner of his mouth. A gesture I was quickly learning to mean that bad things were coming.

"I'd heard rumors," he said after a moment. "But I hadn't thought they were true. All these years . . ." He opened his eyes, and I saw madness there. "Looks like it's your lucky day, witch. You're too valuable to sell." I noticed the crowd around us shifting restlessly in the stands. I wondered how many of them heard what Lucifer said. That's how many people we'd have after us if we got out of here.

Something told me that bastard knew what he was doing.

"What am I?" Nathalie asked, seemingly unable to help herself.

Lucifer snorted. "I think I'll keep that to myself," he said. "Let you wonder why the Lord of the Under-world finds you worth keeping."

I had to resist the urge to roll my eyes. His mega-lomaniac personality was more grating than most of these alpha assholes. Must be because he's a demon. They were the worst of the worst.

"Continue the fights," Lucifer said lazily. "Me and my . . . toys have conditioning to do."

My stomach turned at what being called a toy implied.

Lucifer turned on his heel, saying over his shoulder, "Come with me."

Both Nathalie and I shared a look, and then we followed.

Lucifer walked with his back to us. The fluorescent lights of the hallways were a welcome reprieve from the high-intensity spotlights of the arena.

I mouthed, *are you okay?*

She nodded then mouthed back, *you?* The cautious glance she shot from me to Lucifer told me where her mind had gone.

I'm fine, I said.

She lifted an eyebrow. *Are you?*

It was an odd thing for her to ask me when I should be the one asking her. Nathalie didn't look the sort to kill on a whim and think little of it. Then again, the world had changed from what it had been twenty years ago. It was dog-eat-dog, and in order to survive, sometimes you had to do bad things.

Before I could respond or think on it anymore, Lucifer said, "Anders, find my pussy cats. Let them know I have a job for them."

"Yes, sir," Anders said from several feet away. I leaned to the side to look around for Lucifer, who had stopped in front of a door.

I wrinkled my nose. "Pussy cats?" I said, incredulous to hear a grown man speak like that, let alone a feared demon king.

The door opened. Lucifer motioned for us to enter. "You'll see," he purred.

I stepped inside, Nathalie following close behind me. It wasn't the room I'd woken up in, but it was similar. White couches, slate floors, dim lighting. There was just one more thing.

A king-sized bed.

My heart skipped a beat, and I had to slow my breathing to lower my pulse just enough that I wasn't at risk of flipping right then and there. The door closed behind me.

I whirled around, uncertain of what I was going to do to him if he tried what I thought he was going to—but Lucifer wasn't there. It was just Nathalie and I, in a giant room with a closed door.

We stared at each other. There was a lot I wanted to say. A lot that I was questioning. But the words I settled on were, "You got balls, Nat."

She cracked a smile, despite her split lip. "I'm not the one that spit on him."

I snorted. "Yeah, well, it wasn't one of my finer moments . . ."

We stood there awkwardly. I brushed a hand through my hair, all the way down my long ponytail to the ends. They looked like pure spun gold beneath the ambient lighting.

"I'm sorry I didn't tell you the full truth of my powers," she said. I guess we were talking about the elephant in the room now. "I'm normally weak, but when I'm not . . ."

"You're a fucking bomb?" I finished for her. She pressed her lips together, and I sighed. "Look, we all got secrets, it just so happens both of ours have to do with being freaks that have weird magic." I laughed under my breath, a dark little huff.

"Maybe we can use that to get out of here, since I got caught too." She looked around the room with a renewed curiosity, but I knew there was no way out except through that door. Lucifer wouldn't be stupid enough to put us in a room he thought we could escape. Not when he was dead set on believing I was the key to finding his missing atma, not to mention his keen interest in whatever Nathalie actually was.

She opened the second door and flipped on the light. It was a bathroom, one large enough for an orgy. She sighed in disappointment.

"The plan is still on," I said. "At least for now. He's coming."

Nathalie paused in her snooping. She frowned. A pucker formed between her brows. "How—"

She didn't get to finish her question before a knock came at the door.

It opened without either of us getting it.

A woman dressed in black patent leather lingerie

stepped inside. She had caramel skin and shiny black hair. Two black cat ears poked out of her head of hair. She smiled seductively and strolled into the room like she owned it. Behind her, another woman with the same face and black cat ears walked in. She was wearing a Catholic schoolgirl outfit, complete with the knee-high socks and pigtails.

"Look at them, so shocked. It's like they've never seen a shifter succubus before," the second one purred.

The first one snapped her fingers, and several large men came in bringing a rolling cart of clothes and several utility cases. They lined it up against the empty wall and then left the way they came. Neither Nat nor I said anything until the door clicked shut behind them.

"I call the blonde," the leather dominatrix said. Her long black tail swished behind her. "Her legs will be magnificent."

Catholic schoolgirl groaned. "You always get the good ones."

"You spend too long flaunting yourself, and I don't want to be on the other end of one of Lucifer's punishments." Dominatrix walked right up to me. With her tall heels, we stood eye to eye. Her eyeliner was painted on to perfection, accentuating bright green cat eyes. One of her ears twitched.

"Lucifer wants you prepped and ready for his

party tonight. He's going to show you off. If you behave, the humiliation will be minimal. If you don't, he'll make an example of you—and me." She lifted a hand to touch my face, and I took a step back.

"What exactly does that mean?"

Dominatrix sighed. "Do you really want me to go into all the ways I've seen him punish newbies for disobedience? It's a long list."

I pressed my lips together, reminding myself I couldn't just bust out of here. Not yet. Ronan would show, and I needed him to deal with Lucifer.

Which meant I had to play along.

"Prepped and ready for a party. I'm going to take a wild guess that he wants us dressed like you two, given the rack of ridiculousness over there?" I thrust my chin toward it. Dominatrix smiled.

"Bingo. The nicer you play, the sooner we'll be done."

I eyed Nathalie, who was being poked and prodded by the Catholic schoolgirl. The irony of her outfit given Lucifer's history with the church might have been amusing under other circumstances.

"All right, but I want food. We both do." I motioned to Nat. "And she needs cold medicine. I can't imagine she'll be much fun if she's dripping snot everywhere."

Dominatrix inclined her head. "I can do that. Now I'm going to need you to strip and shower. No offense, but you smell like week-old roadkill. There are towels in the bathroom. I need to see what I'm working with, so don't dress in those clothes again. Just come out naked." She wrinkled her nose at my smell. I shrugged. Being kidnapped and drugged did that to people.

Dominatrix kitty gave me a look as if to say, "get going."

I huffed under my breath and went into the bathroom, closing the door behind me.

This next part was going to be the hardest.

The riskiest.

And it was only my desire to get it all over with that let me strip and step into the shower. I turned the water on, and a cold downpour drenched me. I shivered. The water warmed.

My hands were mechanical in their movements as I washed my hair twice, and then my body. The hot spray was pounding into my back when the bathroom door opened.

"Food is here," one of the pussy cats said. I wasn't sure which, given I couldn't see them through the steamed glass wall of the shower.

"I'll be out in a sec."

The door closed, and I flipped the nozzle off. Water dripped down my body in rivulets. I wrung my hair out three times on the shower floor before opening the foggy glass door. Dew drops of steam condensed on the mirror over the sink. They ran down the length of it, creating streaks where I could see slivers of myself.

I stood there, naked, staring at the intertwining black vines around my neck. The markings changed as they descended my chest, shaping around my breasts, and running over either side of my ribs. They covered my shoulders and most of the way down both arms.

If Lucifer saw them, he would know.

It was enough to make me want to call off this plan. Just give myself to the magic and light the entire place up. See if the white fire that I conjured in rage really was enough to kill him.

Knowing Aeshma was his atma, though . . . it made me pause.

Ronan had said my fire could kill almost anything, but it didn't kill him because of our bond. What if I had some sort of bond with Lucifer that was leftover from Aeshma?

What if it couldn't kill him? What if *I* couldn't?

I needed Ronan, though he didn't know it.

I needed him to deal with Lucifer, and with any luck, Lucifer would deal with him.

So I dried myself with a towel and wrapped it tight around me.

Then I stepped out into the room.

Nathalie sat cross-legged on the couch. She took a

long drink of some amber liquid from a cup and groaned. "Sasha, this is *divine*." Catholic schoolgirl giggled beside her. She was holding a teapot. "Jasmine tea. Lucifer imports it just for us."

Across from them, Dominatrix stood, piling food from a cart onto the long coffee table. White meat chicken breasts covered in some kind of gravy with mushrooms sat on one plate. Roasted green beans, mashed potatoes, fresh fruit, and cake were also among the choices. My mouth watered.

It had been a long time since I'd had a real good meal. After the Magic Wars, fresh food became astronomically expensive. I had to be careful in buying it, but I couldn't bring myself to live on processed stuff alone. I splurged where I could even if it cost an arm and a leg, but when retirement and taxes didn't exist, and vacations were a thing of the past, it was more than worth it.

I considered myself better off than most humans, but food like this, I hadn't had it since I was a kid. I guess there were perks to owning the New Chicago Underworld.

Even your slaves could eat like kings and queens of old.

Three heads turned toward me.

Of the three, it was only Nathalie that eyed my brands.

As if she were starting to put together what they meant. What I was. Who I am.

I tucked the towel under my arms and walked toward the buffet of food.

A pile of clean glass plates and actual silverware sat on the cart. I took one and piled chicken and green beans on my plate. If I could eat my weight in it, I would.

"You should try the tea," Nathalie said, blowing on hers. "It's really good."

I nodded, while taking my first bite of gravy-smothered chicken.

I could have orgasmed on the spot.

My eyes closed, and I savored the way it melted in my mouth. I was never a foodie, in the traditional sense. I ate because my body needed food, and if I'd grown up in a different America, during a different time, I might also be different. But even not being one, I could treasure it. Processed food tasted like shit by comparison.

"Eat up," Dominatrix said. "When you're done, I'll dress you, and then we'll start on your hair and makeup."

"You're up, Nat," Catholic schoolgirl said.

They were getting awfully cozy.

"Sure, sure," Nat said. "Just one more sip." She gave the cat-eared woman an affectionate grin and took a long drink before setting her mug down. She stood up and went to the bathroom. The door shut, and I heard the water turn on.

Silence settled over the three of us while I ate.

The cat twins alternated between silently sharing looks and staring at me.

I had eaten two chicken breasts, half the green beans, and a portion of fruit when Dominatrix finally said, "Your tattoos are interesting."

"Mhmm," I hummed, starting in on my third serving of chicken.

"I've only seen ones similar to them once before," she continued. I paused in my eating and set down the fork.

When I lifted my eyes, they were both staring at me with knowing looks.

"Are we going to have a problem?" I asked, reaching for a napkin to wipe my mouth.

"Has Lucifer seen them?" she asked. There was a new light in her eyes. A dangerous kind.

I noted when picking up the utensils that knives weren't among them. Not even butter knives. I could do a lot with a fork, though. If I needed to. I placed my hand next to it, but didn't pick up just yet. "No."

The cat twins nodded like they expected as much.

"It'll be difficult to find a dress that covers them," the Dominatrix said slowly. "But I think I can."

My lips parted. "Why?"

She gave me a bitter smile. "Why are you here?"

Secrets. It's crazy how mine were displayed on my skin like the pages of a book. For a decade I'd worn turtlenecks and kept my flesh a secret from those that might know. My only partners were humans who were clueless, and they'd just assumed I liked tattoos.

"He thinks I betrayed him," I said.

"That doesn't answer the question," Catholic schoolgirl called Sasha said. She crossed her lean legs and put her arms over the back of the couch. "Why are you here? If you are what we think you are . . ." She trailed off and Dominatrix picked up. "You could kill him. Couldn't you?"

Were we really having this discussion?

"If I say yes," I paused, and lifted an eyebrow.

"I might be able to find a dress that hides those marks," Dominatrix said with a tilt of her head.

"And if I say no?"

"Why would we stick our necks out, then?" Sasha said, tilting her head as well. It was eerie.

I sighed. When they put it that way . . . "There's a chance I can."

They both smiled. "That's good enough for us," they said in unison. Dominatrix extended a hand to me. To help me up. To bargain.

I'd made a lot of dumb bargains that led to this point.

I wasn't sure if this would be another one, but I didn't have a lot of options.

I took her hand, and she smiled as I got to my feet.

"Now, let me see you." She pulled at the towel and I let her. It dropped to my feet, and Sasha let out a whistle.

"If I thought you wouldn't kill us afterward, I'd try to bang on that bed over there." Unlike her vulgar sister, the Dominatrix walked around me in a circle, cataloguing me with a methodical interest.

"You two seem to have it good here with Lucifer. Why do you want him dead?" I asked.

Dominatrix stepped away from me to go rummage through the clothing rack. "Do you know why he calls us his pussy cats?" she asked from across the room.

"Given how you both look, I assume he enjoys fucking you," I said.

"Bingo," she answered. I wasn't sure if it was in response to what I said, or her discovery of the sleek black number she'd just pulled off the rack. "Sasha and I are half cat shifter and half succubus. Our father was an incubus that raped our mother, and she gave us up when we were born."

"That's shitty," I said. Her tail twitched.

"It is," they said in unison.

"We bounced around as orphans until we were thirteen. We were caught and sold here in the Under-world. Lucifer bought us and made us into his pussy cat girls." She spat the title like it was poison in her mouth. "We fuck him however and whenever he wants. We prepare women like you. And if those women don't behave . . . he isn't gentle."

"Mind you," Sasha said salaciously, "I prefer it when he's not gentle."

I shuddered. "I'm assuming I don't want to know."

"You don't," they agreed. Sasha smiled, and it was both seductive and broken. As if two sides of her were at war.

Dominatrix cat girl came back, holding out the little black number. I grabbed a handful of the cloth in my hand. It was soft, and smoother than silk, as it ran through my fingers. "No bra. I'll give you a thong. That should make him happy enough."

I stalled for words. Unfamiliar with anyone helping me. Certainly not supes.

"Thank you," I said softly.

"You're welcome. Now get dressed. Lucifer is too arrogant to put cameras in his rooms, but if we take too long preparing you, he'll come looking."

Not needing to be told twice, I shimmied into the dress.

23

Even I could admit I looked like sex on a stick when the twins were done with me.

At least until I walked. Then I hobbled like a one-legged crone with a crutch. Being as tall as I was, and then adding six-inch heels to the mix, I felt like a strong wind could blow me over.

"Stand up," Sienna, the Dominatrix, chided. "You're hugging the railing like it's going to save you."

"That's because it is," I said under my breath.

My grip tightened on the rail as I looked over the most notorious club in the Underworld. Above us there was no ceiling. Only a full moon and thin clouds drifting through. Despite it being December in New Chicago, it wasn't cold. We had magic to thank for that.

Below me, the club sat at different levels in an odd

layout. Concrete platforms sectioned it off, up and down in large portions. A heavily stocked bar was next to the door, and music played, but I couldn't tell where it was coming from.

The Seventh Circle, as it was called, was in full swing tonight.

"It's time," Sasha said, as she strode down the staircase before us, a seductive smile painted on her face as she greeted the club. I reached up to run a hand over my sleek ponytail. My brands were covered, but that's about all that was in the skintight dress. They'd oiled my long legs after waxing them and then taught me how to walk in the godforsaken shoes. To think women wore these by choice back before the world went to shit.

On the floor, a figure dressed in white stood apart from everyone else. One hand in his pocket, and the other holding a crystal glass with amber liquid, surveying the club. As if sensing my gaze, he lifted his head and his golden eyes met mine.

Lucifer.

My target. My ex-boss. My temporary master, for the evening.

I let go of the railing when nails dug into my forearm. Beside me, Nathalie was dressed as a slutty cheerleader. Sasha had wanted to put her in a maid's outfit, but Nat wasn't a fan of the sheer top that showed off her boobs. They compromised on the cheer outfit that strapped them to her chest and kept them hidden, even if the skirt was short enough to see up it if she leaned forward, or in any direction, for that matter. She also wore heels, except she didn't look like a baby giraffe in them.

We continued our descent, and between Nathalie's death grip on my arm and my hold on the railing, I made it without breaking my neck. It amazed and infuriated me that I could face down vampires and werewolves and witches, but it was fucking shoes that had the best shot of taking me out.

At the bottom of the platform, I wanted to thank the ground for not being stairs, but that white-clad figure was moving toward us.

"Piper," he said huskily. "You look *ravishing*." A bolt of need shot through me at the sheer sound of his voice, and I knew without a doubt it was magic. My knees nearly buckled, but somehow, I remained upright.

He extended his arm, and I didn't want to take it. I wanted to light his ass on fire and watch it burn. But judging by the mad glee in his eyes, he was waiting for any opportunity to exert his power over me.

I took his arm.

"Nathalie," he said, with no less heat in his voice. "I might have you for dessert." He extended his other arm, and she took it, somehow managing not to gag.

Bile climbed up my throat, but I swallowed it down.

Then the show began.

He walked us through the club, and the crowd parted. Eyes followed us everywhere we went. Whispers of the human slave and the Le Fay witch that won the pit fight—and that we now belonged to him.

He didn't introduce us to anyone because he didn't have to.

Everyone knew who Lucifer was.

And now, they knew who we were.

Or so they thought.

The black dress had done well to hide my brands. With long sleeves and a higher neckline, it might have been skintight, but it wasn't see-through.

We approached a platform, a solid foot lower than the one we were on. I slowed. Lucifer tightened his grip on me. He stepped down with fluid grace, and Nathalie followed, only slightly more human in her movements. I twisted, trying to lower myself gingerly.

A dark chuckle escaped him.

He released Nathalie, then pulled on my arm.

I lost my balance and went tumbling forward, but his strong body wrapped around me. He pulled me into his embrace, and the scents of blood and sex washed over me. I swallowed, going still. My damned heartbeat was going to give out before the night's end and blow our whole plan.

Where was Ronan and his stalkerness when I needed it?

"Mmm," Lucifer hummed against my cheek. "You smell like smoke and roses and Aeshma. My favorite."

"What does Aeshma smell like?" I asked because I didn't know what else to say to that. I certainly wasn't going to thank him.

"War," he said quietly. "And rage. You can't smell it because it's magic. Only a demon can scent rage."

He released me as quickly as he'd pulled me to him. Lucifer locked one of his arms through mine, and took Natalie's, then continued forward as if nothing had happened.

He led us to a section in the back of the club. Somewhere that was quieter. The people were few and far between, but the magic was stronger. On every table, sticks like incense burned. I knew better, though, when the need was clawing through my body like an untamable beast. My palms sweat. Goose-bumps broke out over my arms. The hair on the back of my neck prickled when we came to a stop beside a section of couches.

Three people were seated. A woman with long blue hair and black eyes, along with two mostly naked males at her feet.

"Tatiana," Lucifer said with a drawl of delight.

"My lord," she hummed. Tatiana stood and

lowered her head. Both her men, which I assumed were slaves given the collars around their necks, bowed, flattening themselves to the ground.

Lucifer seemed pleased with her display, and said, "Please, my dear, take a seat. Let us talk like . . . friends."

She lifted her head and then dipped it in thanks, but still waited for him to take a seat opposite of her before sitting herself. Lucifer dragged both Nathalie and I down with him, and then lifted his arms to rest at the back of the couch. Magic oozed from his pores at this proximity, and my breath was becoming shallow.

Nathalie looked like she was handling it better than me, but still not well. My . . . affliction made magic and its side effects worse. More pronounced.

I panted softly, and my fingers curled to bite into my palms.

I let myself think back to a decade ago. To what I did. To what happened after.

Images flashed through my mind, and the heat cooled.

But my anger didn't. That was only beginning to surface.

Lucifer lifted the hand to hail down a servant walking around with a tray. The man paused in his steps and leaned forward, inclining his head as he presented the items on the silver platter.

"My lord," the server said solemnly, echoing Tatiana's words from only moments ago.

Lucifer didn't respond as he took a cigar from the selection. The servant made scarce quickly. I didn't see a lighter around, but when he snapped his fingers and a small flame appeared on the tip of his thumb, I was reminded of a time not long ago.

When I sat at a booth in his casino and scolded Anders for trading three days of his life to buy that magic. Now I was wondering if Lucifer was who he'd bought it from.

The Demon King of the Underworld put the cigar to his lips and inhaled, blowing out through his nose.

"Tell me about the shipment," he said, after a moment.

It only took a moment of hearing her speak that I figured out what the shipment was.

People. Young boys and girls, to be specific.

"None of them are older than twelve," she said. "A few are shifters. Only one fae. A girl. She'll fetch a nice price." Tatiana ran a hand through one of her slave's hair. She did it absentmindedly, like how one would pet a dog.

"Any succubi?" he asked, taking another puff from the cigar.

I wrinkled my nose at the musky smell of it. Whatever it was, it was strong, and had magic woven in.

"No," she said.

He dabbed the end of the cigar in the ashtray and hummed under his breath. "Good."

Good?

There were only a few reasons I could think of any kind of shipment like that, and none of them were *good*.

Yet, he was happy there were no succubi.

I thought back on the pussy cats and frowned.

Before I could blank my face, Lucifer lifted an eyebrow in my direction. "Something to say, toy?"

I scowled at the name. "No."

"No?" he asked, mockingly.

"Yes."

He narrowed his eyes, then leaned in. "What are you thinking about, Piper? What is going through that mind of yours that made you frown?"

Magic coated his words, and if I really fought, I knew I could overcome it.

But this wasn't something worth fighting for.

"I'm confused about how someone trafficking children is happy there aren't any succubi."

He didn't say anything for a moment, and Tatiana had grown quiet as well.

"You really think me as horrible as the legends say, don't you?"

He didn't use magic this time, and I wondered if

that was because he didn't truly want the answer. I gave it to him anyway.

"Yes."

Lucifer leaned back and snorted. "Tatiana, meet my new toys, Piper and Nathalie," he said, motioning to each of us with a turn of his head.

"They must be new," she said diplomatically. A nice way of saying I wasn't broken in yet.

Lucifer grinned. "They are. Perhaps it's time for a little show of obedience, then. What say you?"

Tatiana smiled and my stomach plummeted.

Lucifer rubbed his hands together in anticipation.

"Nathalie, go sit on Piper's lap. I want you both to give me and Tatiana a show."

I blinked.

He couldn't be serious. He wanted . . . a tease? A show? A—

I was jarred from my own surprise when Nathalie straddled my lap. She reached up to curl her arms around my neck. I felt her back bow as her front pressed into mine.

She loomed closer, and there was a look of apology in her eyes.

Was she apologizing for this shitty fucking plan I never should have agreed to? Or what came after?

I wasn't sure, but the next moment her lips pressed against mine.

Let it be known, I wasn't a prude. Most of my

fuck buddies had been men, but I did have an occasional dalliance with a woman. They gave better head than any guy I'd been with, so kissing her wasn't unpleasant, really. She was warm and soft. Her hair easily slipped through my fingers, and the smooth skin and hard muscles of her thighs were attractive.

She was a pretty girl. A smart girl. Not my usual type, but that wasn't the issue. There was only one simple problem.

I wasn't into her. At all.

Maybe it was because the first time I'd really seen her was at a demon summoning. Or maybe it was because I kidnapped her, and then she got sick. There was also the little issue of her being a witch. I preferred my partners more . . . human.

But Lucifer asked for a show.

And she was a great actress.

So when Nathalie kissed me, I kissed her back. Our lipstick smeared. She smelled like raspberries and juniper. It was a sweet scent. Pleasant enough for me to easily lean into.

Her fingers knotted my hair. I gripped her thighs roughly, pulling her against me.

She made a soft noise that enticed me, and I broke our kiss.

My lips trailed her jaw and down the slender column of her throat. I pressed a soft kiss there and my eyes slanted open. Tatiana was absorbed in our show. One slave at her feet had moved between her legs, eating her out. The other had turned to fucking that one from behind.

The muscles of his backside went taut as he thrust into the other man.

As far as situations to land myself in, a demon orgy was pretty high on the list of places I didn't want to be. Not much could make it worse.

Movement behind Tatiana made me frown. I pulled back from Nathalie just a fraction as a sense of knowing came over me. My blood recognized him a second before I did.

Ronan stepped out of the crowd.

24

BLACK FIRE REFLECTED in his gaze.

My body froze. Nathalie instantly stopped what she was doing, as if sensing the change in me.

The music in the Seventh Circle still boomed. People danced. People drank. Tatiana was still writhing as she was being pleasured, and the men fucking were still chasing release. I almost wondered if I was the only one that could see him and the smoke drifting in wisps from his suit . . . if I was the only one that could feel his power growing, amassing, the volatile churning beneath his flesh form.

Then Lucifer spoke.

"Harvester." For once, there was none of the pleasantness. None of the mania. He was ice, but fire was upon him, bearing down with its smoldering heat.

Ronan stopped behind the couch Tatiana was on.

He let out a dark chuckle. My skin pebbled.

"Lucifer," he said. "I should have known. Still pining for Aeshma? It's been a few thousand years, hasn't it?"

Nathalie pulled away, and I turned sideways to eye the demon next to me. His lips were pulled back in the makings of a snarl. Hatred burned in his cold eyes. His magic snapped in the air like a whip. Desire burned in me that was not my own.

And yet it was.

"She was my atma," Lucifer said softly. "Mine."

Ronan smiled cruelly, and that wickedness pulled at the threads of my careful composure. Adrenaline was flooding my system.

There was something in what Lucifer said that made me pause, though.

Was.

Not is.

"I see you've figured it out," Ronan said softly. "So why is *my* atma sitting beside you?"

Lucifer stilled, then his gaze slid sideways. First to Nathalie, then to me.

For the first time, true surprise that he couldn't mask filled his features.

"That's not possible," he whispered. The words were meant for Ronan, but his eyes were on me. "Piper is mine now, and I'm not letting you corrupt her like you did Aeshma."

If it were possible for fireworks to explode in my head and temporarily blind me, it would have happened then.

Lucifer knew. He *knew* Aeshma was gone.

Dead.

But he kept me under the guise of finding her.

What's more, *he* was claiming Ronan would corrupt me. The irony wasn't lost on me.

Lucifer. The Lord of the Underworld. The Morningstar. The Devil.

He was worried about Ronan *corrupting* me.

There was history there. Did I dare hope it was enough so it would come to blows?

Yes. Yes, I did.

Lucifer's arm curled around my shoulders, pulling me in.

Nathalie tightened her hold on me. Her hands slipped from my hair to my shoulders.

"She carries traces of Aeshma, but she is not Aeshma. You're confused, Brother."

Brother? Wait a second. He was—

My head tilted to the side as dark power began building within him. I sensed it from the little bit of blood that mingled between us. He was prepared to end everything. The club. The city of New Chicago. Certainly Lucifer, if it meant getting to me. It was enough to distract me from learning both of the alphaholes being related.

Sixteen-year-old Piper would have thrown herself at him like the lovesick, romantic fool she was. I tried dating vampires and getting them to change me. I went looking for shifters on full moons. I wanted eternity and power because I viewed those things as safety.

But power came at terrible costs.

Last, I went to the witches for it, and they gave it to me.

That's why I was here now. That decision was the fucking gift that kept on giving.

"One never confuses the scent of their atma. We know it in our blood. Our *soul*. Her magic sings to me. I will not give her up."

Ronan sighed, then reached up to undo his cuff links.

"That's unfortunate."

Lucifer frowned. Nathalie's nails bit into my skin. The second my blood welled beneath the black dress, both demons froze. Their nostrils flared. They looked at me.

The hunger in their gazes was enough to scare the shit out of me.

All hell broke loose.

Nathalie tried to pull us to the side, off the couch. Lucifer was faster. He grabbed me roughly, pulling me into him. My waist twisted and body contorted as my face was pressed into his collarbone. The arms around my shoulders became a steel band, keeping me there whether or not I wanted it.

"You made a mistake coming here, Brother," Lucifer spat the familial term at Ronan. "I've been on earth a long time. I'm not the weak angel you remember."

I couldn't see much with the way my face was smashed against his chest and trying to pull away wasn't getting me anywhere. My heart started to race, and this time I didn't attempt to calm it. I just had to hope my other self was enough to get me out of here.

If the crash didn't claim me first.

I writhed, and the arm tightened further, threatening to crush my ribs.

"Just remember, Luci, I gave you a way out."

Magic thickened, and I knew I had seconds at most to make my move before Ronan and Lucifer would fight. Resorting to the only action I had left that might work on him, I opened my mouth.

Then I bit him.

My teeth sank deep into his flesh.

The scent of his blood hit me as the first drops welled against my teeth. Lucifer groaned, but it wasn't in pain.

Blood touched my tongue, and the ichor consumed me. It tasted different from Ronan's. Like bliss. Like the best sex of my life. Desire clawed at me.

Heat enveloped me as ice tried to crawl through

my veins. My inner fire fanned hotter. Brighter. It started to burn with a dull ache in my chest.

I shuddered, taking another long pull from his neck. My senses heightened, and the feel of him pressed against me blurred my racing heartbeat with the sounds and smells of the club.

It thumped in my ears. Faster. Faster. Fa—

Silence.

My heart stopped.

And then came the rage.

I shuddered as magic poured through my veins. Strength that no human or supernatural could compete with filled me. Fire touched my vision, staining it red.

I reeled back and Lucifer couldn't stop me.

Despite my great efforts, his blood called to me, making me pause, not even for a full second. I didn't have a chance to process the all-consuming need I saw in his expression. A hand grabbed at my own and pulled.

I looked away, and the trance was broken. Nathalie stood there tugging at me, like I was an immovable statue, but by god she was going to try anyway. I jumped to my feet and ran like my ass was on fire.

Like the beasts of Hell itself were chasing me.

They kind of were.

We darted around the couch, and my longer legs

and enhanced speed quickly overcame hers. The club was packed, but no one seemed to notice us. They were all facing toward Ronan and Lucifer.

We only made it to the first raised platform when magic erupted.

It's a strange thing not seeing something but feeling it in the air.

It shouldn't have a scent, but it smelled like darkness and light. Fire and ice. Chaos and desire.

Lucifer said that humans and supernaturals couldn't smell magic. Only demons.

I tried not to think about that as I dodged a waitress dressed like a pinup girl. There was just one tiny little problem.

The goddamned heels.

My ankle twisted, and a snap took me down. I dropped to one knee, and a shadow of pain lanced through me. It was there, but also distorted, as if I were feeling it through a barrier.

I reached down to take the heel off, and Nathalie dropped to her knees beside me, pulling at my other one.

"You've got a lot of explaining to do when we get out of here," she said under her breath. She was faster at undoing the straps. I got frustrated and pulled, the thin strip of leather ripped in half, and I wrenched my foot out of it.

"*If* we get out of here," I corrected.

Nathalie snorted. She tugged at my hand, and I clambered after her, better now that my own two feet were on solid ground again.

I swore right then and there I was never wearing heels again.

Ever.

Roaring filled my ears even as we got further away from the two demons having a pissing contest over me. I wasn't sure if it was my own blood in my ears, or them. I sure as shit wasn't turning to see.

Racing up the concrete platforms as fast as my legs would carry me, I searched for the door I'd noticed when I'd descended the stairs. We had to get out of the Seventh Circle and into the rest of the Underworld to even stand a chance. Once there, we could find one of the doorways out of here and into the rest of New Chicago.

I pushed myself harder, pulling Nathalie behind me. The exit door loomed, already open, which made it that much easier. We burst through it, landing disoriented in the middle of a street in the Under-world. The buildings were dark, the atmosphere gloomy beneath the full moon. Cold nipped at my bare skin and creeped beneath the piece of fabric I'd been dressed in.

I didn't recognize the location, not that I expected to, given my last trip to the Underworld was over a year ago. "Come on," Nathalie said, tugging me to

the right. I didn't have the time to question her. I
followed, and we ran.

How she was doing it in heels was beyond me.

"We'll never make it to the doorway in time," she
panted. "We need to find a place to lie low and see if
either of them make it out alive."

"If we don't get to the doorway, it's all over. You
saw them. They'll never let me go, and if I'm in the
Underworld, they'll lock it down," I said, breathing
much easier than her.

"That's *if* they make it out."

My stomach turned at her comment. I ignored it.

"That's a big gamble," I said. "We need to get
back to the car and get the hell out of here. Fuck
them both. If I have to run for the rest of my life, I
will, but I won't be captured and held hostage by a
demon. You can either come with me, or this ends
now."

She sighed, then threw her head back and
groaned.

"We'd better hurry up, then. They're going to
assume we're going for the doorway."

She wasn't wrong, but I didn't say it.

Maybe it was stubborn. Maybe it was dumb. But I
was not letting myself get trapped in the Underworld
with two demons that believed I was their atma.

The further we got from the Seventh Circle, the
less magic tainted the air. It was quieter in this part of

the Underworld. I wasn't sure if that also meant it was seedier. Nathalie took two lefts before slowing. She bent at the waist, and I was forced to stop, not knowing where we were.

"We have to keep going," I said.

She nodded, then thrust her chin toward her feet. "Shoes," she panted. "I need them off." I knelt at her feet and ripped the tall heels to shreds. My rage was beginning to slip. We didn't have time for this.

She was just starting to move past me when something in my periphery caught my attention. A rustle. A slight shift in the shadows.

I swallowed down the bile rising in my throat.

The scents of blood and sex drifted over me.

"There's a doorway just at the end of this street," Nathalie said. When I didn't get up, she paused mid-stride and turned. "Piper?"

"It's too late," I said softly. "He's here."

25

RONAN

Luci claimed he was not the same angel after all these years. That he had changed. But from where I stood, ten thousand years passed in the blink of an eye and he was still running.

No, that's not right. Chasing. Her. My atma.

He ran from Aeshma when she rejected him. Lucifer tore a rift between our world and this one, then jumped through it. He couldn't handle the sting of her rejection, or that he became a pariah afterward. So he came to this plane and painted himself in a new light.

The Morningstar. The Devil. The Ruler of Hell.

That last one made me chuckle, and the supernaturals surrounding me took notice. Unease swept through the crowd as I began rolling up my sleeves.

This was my favorite suit. It would be a shame to ruin it.

"I realize that you are all blood-bonded to my miserable little brother, but if any of you believe you can fight it, then kneel now, and you will be spared."

No one moved.

Not one single inch.

I sighed.

This was going to get messy. Lucifer had already taken off, stepping through the light to chase after Piper. I needed to get her before he ruined everything.

I didn't care what he said. Piper was not his *anything*. She was mine.

And he wouldn't take her from me.

A quick sweep of the club told me there were hundreds of souls, all prepared to be a barrier between us.

But my brother underestimated me. While he'd spent the last ten thousand years running, hiding, and lying through his teeth—I became the Harvester.

Hundreds of souls were nothing to me.

And I proved it with a snap of my fingers.

26

A LAUGH ECHOED through the empty alley, equal parts mad and flirtatious.

I turned in circles, but it was all brick walls and boarded-up windows. A shitty metal stairwell went up one building on the left side of the street. The only source of light apart from the moon was a broken lamp flickering in and out. It reflected off the shallow puddles and the slivers of glass that peeked through the boards blocking the windows.

"We can still run," Nathalie said. "We can make it—"

"If we run, he catches you too. The crash is coming, Nat. I'm going down. Running for the doorway was my choice, let me pay for it. Leave me." The words came out in broken fragments. My rage may have been fading, but I still had some fight in me yet.

I wouldn't be taken.

But that didn't mean it wasn't my only option.

If I could escape Ronan twice, I could escape Lucifer.

"I'm not leaving you," she said, standing her ground at my side.

"Then you're a fucking idiot because if I didn't know he'd get me anyway, I'd leave you."

Hurt crossed her face before she buried it under anger.

"You don't mean that," she said. "You're such an asshole, and ever since I met you, I question my own sanity, but I see you, Piper. I see who you really are, and I'm not leaving you here to get taken. We either make it out together, or not at all."

I wanted to rip my own hair out. She was infuriating.

Why couldn't she just take the easy way? Why did she have to force my hand?

"Goddamnit Nat, why can't you just—"

A soft tsking brought my words to a grinding halt.

Lucifer walked out of thin air. Literally. Blood smudged his white suit and neck, but he didn't look any worse for wear beyond that. How was that possible?

"Where's Ronan?" I asked.

The pleasant mask turned brittle under his anger. "Fun fact about being a demon on earth. Nothing has magic unless you give it magic. I was the first demon here, ten thousand years ago. The first to learn. One drop of my blood and they change into a supernatural. That I own. My club was filled with them. They're keeping the Harvester busy."

The way none of them tried to stop me suddenly made sense.

He'd already sicced them on Ronan.

"Nathalie, I *need* you to leave."

"No—"

Lucifer laughed, temper cooling once more. His mood swings were giving me whiplash. "You're a conundrum, Piper. You don't trust her to even know what you are, yet you openly discuss killing me with my own people."

"What's he talking about?" Nathalie asked.

"Nothing," I replied in a hard voice. Lucifer grinned.

"Your hatred of magic has blinded you. It was all too easy for the pussy cats to give you a sad story and gain your trust, yet you won't give it to her. I find this *fascinating*."

"Nathalie—"

"I'm. Not. Leaving," she said in a punctuated voice. "Even if you're a dick. We'll be talking about this later." Her unyielding sense of loyalty was going to get us killed if I didn't buckle.

I didn't want to do this with her present.

I'd already come to grips with the fact that I wouldn't kill her. I couldn't. I might be an asshole, and prejudiced, and downright mean sometimes, but I wasn't the kind of person that killed someone who stuck their neck out for me.

Our strange partnership started as a kidnapping, but the only reason it became more was because she chose to trust me. To help me. To save me.

I wouldn't kill her, but she'd die all the same if I did nothing. We both would.

"Come," Lucifer said, beckoning me forward. In this state I was so much more susceptible to that honeyed voice. I let the magic urge me on and used it to fuel me.

To fuel my rage. *My* magic.

A decade of festering hate rose to the surface as I walked across broken concrete.

"I'm going to let you both walk out of here tonight. Alone."

"You must really think I'm stupid if you think I'll fall for that," I snapped. He reached out and brushed the back of his fingers over my cheek.

"Actually, I think you're quite smart. Enough so to know this won't end well if I try to take you. My supernaturals are holding off the Harvester, but it won't be long before he joins us. Once he catches up, there will be a fight. One of us will win, and that person will never let you out of their sight again."

I jerked my head back, and he didn't seem bothered by it.

"I'm not a bird to be caged."

"I know. That's why I'm going to set you free. For now." He leaned in and ran the tip of his thumb over my bottom lip. "But first, I'm going to bite you."

Lucifer grabbed my arm before I could react. He spun me around, pressing my back to his chest. I felt his lips and saw Nathalie's wide-eyed surprise.

Then he sank his teeth into my neck.

At first it hurt. But the pain was only a small prick compared to the lust that filled me. My core turned aching. My legs became heavy. My skin was hot, then cold. Goosebumps broke out across my flesh.

Ice trailed down my stomach and between my legs, filling me with dark desire.

Lucifer groaned, his arms tightening around my waist. I felt him, his magic, his blood, his soul. I felt it all answer to me.

And I *loved* it. This power. This strength. This desire.

But that didn't stop me from burning it all.

I looked Nathalie in the eye as I made my choice. Ronan said another blood-exchange would kill me.

I'm not sure if it would or not, but I was taking him down either way.

White fire erupted.

It started at my shoulders and travelled down to my hands. I clamped them down on his arms that held me. The fire covered my chest and was just starting down my abdomen when he pulled back and tried to pull away. Blood dripped from my neck, and the thin dress went up in flames, showing my body for what it was.

For what I was.

A demon.

I was made, not born, but a demon all the same.

My brands glowed red-hot as I funneled all my rage and resentment with thoughts of my sister. Of the way she looked when I stumbled home from the summoning all those years ago. I'd just consumed Aeshma, and the witches were after me. I had nowhere to go. Bree thought I was stupid. She was so, so angry that I would risk myself—my family—for magic.

We had to run, but we didn't get far.

The witches found us within hours.

They killed my parents first.

Two spells. One for each. Their bodies caught fire, and they burned alive, like the witches of old. When my parents' screams died down and the smell of burnt flesh had filled the air, they turned to me.

Except whatever spell they used to try to kill me missed and hit Bree instead.

She went down. I'll never forget the way her eyes went blank. They closed mid-fall. The sound of her body hitting the ground was the last thing I remembered.

I lost myself to the rage for the first time.

When the red cleared, all that remained was blood and body parts and an unconscious sister who never woke up. She wasn't dead. But she wasn't living either.

I thought of her and my family and the life I should have had. The life *she* should have had, had it not been for my actions.

I'd been told that resentment was anger at another for how they had wronged you, and I had a lot of that aimed at the witches.

But guilt is being angry with yourself. Rage that festers inside you, eating at you like a parasite, an everlasting reminder of what you had done.

For the last decade I ran from it, and from myself.

While it might have been what drove me forward, I never acknowledged it. I certainly didn't think about why it was there. I never let myself *feel* it because it was too painful.

My guilt, my resentment, my own rage had been eating me alive for a decade.

And now, I gave in to it.

I *felt* it all.

And it burned.

From a place so deep inside that I didn't even know it existed; these horrible feelings drew out every last bit of fire. Every flicker of flame. Every spark. Every ember.

Until I couldn't burn anymore.

I let go of Lucifer, or what remained of him, and stumbled forward into the cold, naked as the day I was born. There was no sound in this place outside of the roaring in my ears. My body and my mind detached from each other as I floated in an abyss of pain, even as I kept moving.

I half expected Nathalie to run from me, but she didn't. God this girl, she ran *to* me. She put one arm around my waist and held up half my weight.

We didn't say anything to each other. We just kept walking. Kept moving. It wasn't even until I was at the end of the street that I turned and looked back.

A chill ran through me.

There was a spot in the street that was black and charred. Ashes drifted in the cold wind.

Lucifer wasn't there, but not even for a second did I let myself think he was dead.

It was never that easy. The Devil might be injured and have crawled back to the pit he came from, but he'd be back for his pound of flesh. I was sure of it.

And one way or another, I would be ready.

27

WE STEPPED out of the Underworld. The first flakes of snowfall descended on us. I shivered, and Nathalie held me tighter.

The crash was coming. I felt it deep in my bones, my magic, my soul.

"I won't make it to the car," I said. My words tasted like ash on my tongue.

"I guess it's a good thing we're not going to the car," she replied.

My teeth chattered, preventing me from protesting as Nathalie dragged me halfway down the street. She stopped in front of a thrift store and eased herself away from me. Without looking either way down the road, she brought her elbow up and smashed it into the window.

The glass fractured, breaking apart instantly.

I wrapped my arms around myself as she ripped off her skimpy shirt. She pinched the fabric on either side of the hem and pulled it apart, watching as it unraveled at the crease. She tossed the piece of fabric on the other side before carefully lifting her leg through the window, avoiding the sharp edges. A hiss of pain slipped from between her lips, but she gritted her teeth and kept going. It felt like the longest minutes of my life when she disappeared into the shadows. She came back wearing Crocs and some sort of long skirt over her previous thong-clad ass. In her arms, she carried a bundle of clothing.

"Put your hands on my shoulders," she said, holding out a pair of sweats to help dress me like a child. Normally, I would have complained. I didn't have it in me.

She shucked them up each of my legs and then rolled them at my waist. When she seemed convinced her handiwork would hold, she slipped soft house shoes over my feet. Then she lifted my arms and tugged an oversized hoodie down my top half.

I was still freezing, but at least I wouldn't attract attention as she dragged me through the dark streets of New Chicago. Even in my depleted state, I could tell we were going in the opposite direction of the human neighborhoods where I'd parked the car.

"If you're kidnapping me, I'll shoot you," I mumbled.

Nathalie snorted. "Even after all this you're still talking about shooting me. Why am I not surprised?"

"'Cause I'm an asshole," I said, my words starting to slur. They were broken up with the chattering of teeth as my jaw spasmed from the cold.

"You're not going to hear any disagreement from me," she muttered. She didn't see the faint grin I gave in the dark, but it was there. "It's right around the corner. Can you hold on that long?"

"Can try," I grunted.

"That's all I'm asking for."

Spots danced in my vision. I made it through a door, but everything was hazy. Images faded in and out. Colors danced. My legs shook, locking up every other step.

I fell. But for once, I wasn't terrified of where I'd wake up.

Not that I would tell her that even if I could.

I was an asshole, after all.

I waited there, alone in the dark. For the first time, my memories didn't assault me. Perhaps that's because I'd finally acknowledged them and their exist-ence. Or perhaps, I was just batshit.

They both seemed probable.

It wasn't long before the presence appeared at my

back. I didn't see him, but I felt him. His power. His pull. His very existence demanded my attention. I was the ocean, scrambling to get away from the moon, only to be ripped back every time.

When I didn't turn to face him, he chuckled.

That dark, deep, and lovely sound washed over me. I wished it were like nails on a chalkboard to my ears. But that would make me even more of a liar than I already was.

And I was so damn tired of the lying.

"What do you want, Ronan?"

The chuckle stopped. I felt the predator in him shift at my tone. "Why do you ask me questions you know the answer to?" he mused. "I am not the one that lies. I have been straightforward with you since the very beginning—when you called me out of my world and into this one."

I sighed. "You can't have me. I'm not a bone for you and Lucifer to fight over."

"No, you're not," he agreed. "You're my atma. In your world, shifters have mates, and humans have spouses, vampires have brides, and witches have psychic partners. You are more than all of them to me. Those are simply watered-down imitations of what it means to have an atma."

"You're wrong," I said, turning to face him instead of being the coward I wanted to be. "Being someone's spouse is a choice. Mates and brides and psychic partners don't have that, but wives? Husbands? They choose. That is more than any *bond* that forces itself on people."

Ronan assessed me carefully.

"Choice," he murmured. "That's what you value."

"Yes, and it's what you have not given me."

"If I gave you a choice, you wouldn't even consider it. You'd turn me away because of your prejudice," he pointed out. I shrugged, not denying it.

"I guess it sucks to be you. But chasing me like this? Hounding me like a dog in heat—it won't win me, Ronan. I might not be human anymore, but I was born one. I am human in the ways that matter."

Winter skies and steel shone in his eyes as he considered my words. He was shirtless again, this time in slacks. Smudges of blood smeared on his skin. His brands seemed to pulsate in my presence. As if calling to me.

"Perhaps," he murmured again. "I need to find another way to win you."

"That wasn't an invitation—"

"But it was," he said, smiling with that cruel beauty. "You may not realize it yet, but you're playing this game. I just need to turn the tables."

I stepped forward, opening my mouth to ask him what that meant.

But Ronan disappeared. His body fragmented

into shadows and faded into the darkness of my mind. I sensed his power leaving.

Those parting words, full of promise, unsettled me more than I wanted to admit.

He was planning something. I had no doubt I'd soon know what.

28

A SOFT WARMTH spread through me. I rolled, burying my face deeper into the cool pillow. It smelled like jasmine tea and lilac. I inhaled deeply and then sighed softly.

It took another five seconds for that in-between state of being awake and asleep to shift more toward awake, and reality crashed down. I opened my eyes, and bright, brilliant sunlight assaulted me. I winced, taking in the soft cream walls and the jazz music playing in the background.

My body was stiff as I twisted, trying to sit up. My legs tangled in the blankets. Gravity threatened to pull me back down as a wave of dizziness hit.

"Drink this," Nathalie said from beside me. She passed over a glass of water that was clear and cold;

fat droplets of condensation running down the side of the glass.

I took it between my hands and drank greedily.

At the end I choked, and she took the glass as I coughed roughly.

My ribs ached, and a jackhammer started pounding into my head.

"How long?" I rasped, between breaths.

"Four days," she said, knowing what I was talking about.

The coughing subsided, and I cursed under my breath. I knew it was longer by the hunger and dehydration getting at me, but I didn't think it would be that long. I wondered how many more times it could happen before I wouldn't wake up. Before starvation or dehydration killed me.

It was a somber thought. I pushed it away for now, taking in my surroundings.

I was on a twin-sized bed with an off-white comforter. Behind me, a window spanned a few feet, the long drapes wide open, letting the sun warm me through the pane of glass. There was an antique-looking end table beside me, with crystals and the now empty glass on it. On the other side of the room, a small bookcase had more crystals and knickknacks. Books of all types. Including raunchy romance ones, if the titles were anything to go by. The room was small, and a double set of

French doors with glass panes were wide open, leading into another, larger room with living room furniture.

"Where are we?"

"My apartment," Nat said with a sigh. "You crashed as we were coming through the shop downstairs. I had to drag your ass into the elevator. You're lucky there was an elevator. You weigh a lot more than you look." The last bit was added with a bit of a grin sliding up one side of her face. She was amused. I wasn't.

"Why did you bring me here?"

"Because we were never going to make it to the car, and my apartment is warded. No one will find you here. Not with blood magic. Your demon hasn't shown up either, so I'd guess it probably protects against that too."

I swallowed hard and looked away. The jazz music was subtle, but it filled the awkward silence when I couldn't.

"You saved me," I said eventually.

Nathalie nodded. "And you saved us. I guess we're even now."

I leaned back, titling my head to rest it against the window.

"Lucifer isn't dead," I said. "He'll be back."

She nodded slowly. "I kinda figured as much. Demons seem to be harder to kill than other supes."

She reached out and took my hand before I could yank it away. "But we'll find a way."

I frowned. "We will?"

She snorted. "You can be so dense sometimes. Yes. *We* will. I told you, I'm not leaving you. Not even if you're a—"

"Don't say it."

She tilted her head, and I pushed her hand away. "Why?"

I didn't answer her immediately . . . because I couldn't. "Just . . . don't say it."

"Demon," she said.

"I just said—"

"Demon. Demon. Demon. You're a demon—" I grabbed the pillow from behind my lower back and whacked her in the face with it.

"You're annoying."

She chuckled. "Pot meet kettle. You have a real lack of social skills, you know that? Have you ever actually cracked a smile, or said thank you for anything? You should work on that." I pressed my lips together, and she laughed again. "Look, I'm doing this for you. You're afraid of it, and you shouldn't be."

"I'm not afraid," I argued.

"Then what are you?" she challenged, lifting both eyebrows.

I took a deep breath and exhaled heavily. "Preju-diced. Hateful. Wishing I could still be in denial."

Her expression softened. "I take it you weren't born one."

I shook my head. "I . . . I was made." My mouth was dry again, but this time it was for a whole other reason.

"How does one make a demon?" Nathalie mused, leaning back in her chair. She kicked her feet up onto the end of the bed.

"With a summoning," I said. "At least that's how I was. You know the girl your coven used as a sacrifice?"

She nodded.

"I *was* her. Ten years ago. Claude Lewis led a summoning, and I was chosen as the sacrifice. They told me that I would be able to bargain for power. That I could be made into a supe." I looked at the ceiling as I recounted it because I couldn't look her in the eyes. "Only later did I realize it was all a lie. I survived that summoning on pure dumb luck when I should have died."

"You hate magic," she said. A statement, not a question.

I laughed humorlessly. "People keep saying that. You gotta remember, I was born human. The world changed in a single day, and suddenly I went from being on equal footing to being at the bottom of society. My family . . ." I struggled with this part. To recall those memories. Bittersweet. The best and the worst.

"We were treated horribly. I watched my parents lose their jobs and then struggle to make ends meet. My mom had to sell her body to put food on the table because there was literally no other work for a human woman. She tried to hide it, but the vampire clients she had were rough with her because they could be. It tore my dad apart. Things got better when he helped form human patrol, but it was still difficult. I'd had enough. If I wasn't born equal, then I was going to take power and make myself equal."

"I'm so sorry," Nat said softly.

I shrugged, though I didn't mean it. "It's not your fault."

"Witches were the ones to start the wars. We revealed magic to the world."

I nodded. "Revealing it didn't change whether or not it existed. It was what happened afterward that screwed us over. But that's why I went looking for magic, and eventually I found someone that would give it to me."

"If you were meant to be a sacrifice," she paused. "How did you end up with a demon's magic? Every sacrifice used in a summoning dies. They never even get to bargain for power, and of the people that do, half of them die because the magic doesn't take. Yet you got all of it. How?"

"Honestly? I don't know. Something went wrong. She came forward, but she never fully formed. She and I—we made a link of sorts. It was short, but for that small span of time, I heard her, and I felt her— and then I became her. I never drank Aeshma's blood. I just absorbed all that she was, then the link fizzled, and she died." I shrugged again. "I struggled at first. The magic was a lot to take in. I broke the circle, and the witches were knocked unconscious. I was young and dumb. I went straight home like a child, and then told my parents everything. We tried to get out of town, but it was too late."

"They found you," Nat said quietly. "They killed your parents, didn't they?"

"Yes."

"And Bree?" she prompted.

I lowered my eyes, and when I finally looked back at her, I hated the pity I saw there. I didn't deserve it. I brought this on them. On myself.

"She took a spell meant for me. It put her in some kind of coma. I've been trying to find a way to wake her up for the last decade, but no one knows what spell was used. I didn't even think he was alive until the summoning that night."

"That explains why you bargained with the demon instead of just killing us," she said. "You were hoping he was strong enough his magic could break the spell without killing her."

I nodded. "Claude, Kenneth—whoever he was— he was the source. He knew which spell he'd cast, which meant he could undo it. That's why I tried to send the demon after the rest of you while I got him. But Ronan killed him."

"Ronan?" She frowned.

"The demon from the club," I said. "His name is Ronan, or at least that's what he goes by. Demons wear their true names on their skin."

Her eyes drifted to my form. I was wearing a T-shirt now, but the brands on my arms were still visible.

"I never knew," she said.

"Most don't," I replied. "It was one of the few things I learned from Aeshma before I absorbed her."

"Are your brands the same as hers?" Nat asked.

"I don't know," I said. "But I don't think so. They change, now and then. In the same way a person changes and grows, who we are, our true name does as well." Her eyes seemed to light up, soaking in the little bits of knowledge I was sharing.

"Does your name have a sound? Do the markings mean something?"

"They mean different things, but they're not like letters. They're specific to each of us. Our magic and our souls. My true name has a sound, or multiple, but before you ask—no, I'm not telling you what it is."

She frowned. "Why?"

"Because that's how you control a demon. Truly control them. If you know their name, then you can make them do whatever you want."

She opened, then closed her mouth. "I see. How did you learn your name if it changes?"

"It's hard to explain. I just sort of know. When one of the brands change, so does my name." I shrugged again, not the most comfortable with the topic.

"Thank you for sharing with me," she said.

I shrugged again. "I figure if you run your mouth, I could just shoot you."

She tossed the pillow back at me, and with the tiny pricks of feathers poking at my face, I grinned into it.

"It's not like I have many people to run my mouth to. Besides, you know my secret too. I guess we've both got weird magic."

I snorted. "You blew up that fae chick. I'm not sure weird is the only word I'd use to describe it anymore."

She sighed. "That happens sometimes. Especially when someone uses their magic against me. I just panic, and then it's like this switch flips and I take all their magic and throw it back at them. I don't even know how I do it."

She looked troubled, and if I were a better person, I might have taken her hand and said we'd figure it out.

But I wasn't.

I was an asshole.

"That would have been great to know when we

had that entire conversation about you keeping secrets and shit," I griped. "You could have killed me."

"It's not like I'm the only one," Nat said, but not as defensive as I would have thought. "Besides, when we were in the dressing room, you told me everyone has secrets, and you've been keeping an awful lot yourself."

"Yeah, well, that's when I thought we would die," I deadpanned.

She lifted an eyebrow at me and crossed her arms over her chest, not accepting that for one second.

"Trust goes both ways, Piper. You've been screwed over a lot. You've seen the people you love suffer at the hands of supes. I get that. But it takes both sides to change things. You're stuck with me now, but only you can decide how this is going to go between us."

She gave me an expectant look. I couldn't believe how much had happened in the last two weeks. Truly. If someone had told me I'd be telling my deepest, darkest secrets to a witch of all people, I would have laughed. I certainly wouldn't have thought twice about it.

But Nathalie wasn't just a witch. Hell, she might not even be a witch at all.

And I wasn't just a human. Or a demon. My heart was human, but my body . . . it was remade. What happened in that summoning circle ten years ago changed my life irrevocably.

We were both something else. Something other . . . and maybe together we could find out what.

"Okay," I said eventually.

She frowned and her eyebrows drew together. "Okay?" she asked. "That's the best I get? You *finally* tell me a little bit about you, and we connect, and then—"

"Don't make this weirder than it is," I said, stopping her.

"Ugh," she groaned. "I really can't with you. But fine. Whatever. So how are we going to do this?"

"First, I need a shower. Then, I need food. After that, I need to find a way to get this blood magic tracker removed—"

She made a face, and I paused. "What does that face mean?"

"Well, I, uh . . . I may have had Barry come remove it while you were asleep."

She scratched the back of her head.

"You what—"

"It's not like you're the most reasonable about things. I figured if you were already asleep, it couldn't hurt. Besides, you wanted it done and now it is."

"I cannot believe you right now."

"A thank you will suffice," she said.

I blinked, debating throwing the pillow at her again. "Where's the bathroom?" I said. Kicking her legs off, I scrambled to get out of bed.

"Right around the corner, down the hall, last door at the end." She scooted her chair back to give me room. I was dizzy at first, but pushed past it to get around her and put some space between us. Her living room was cozy, small but stylish. I spotted a kitchen on my way to the bathroom, as well as a few closed doors. I'd have time to snoop later. When I felt less disgusting and could talk to Nathalie without wanting to throw shit at her. That girl really did my head in sometimes.

I paused with my hand on the last door.

She might do my head in, but all things considered, I was lucky to have her. Without her, I'd be dead, and Bree's only chance at waking up would die with me.

"I'm happy I didn't shoot you," I said loudly. It was the closest to a thank you she was going to get.

I heard Nat snort, as if she knew that. Though she was in another room, I heard her whispered reply. "Me too."

29

I touched my fingers to the brand on my chest.

A delicate thorn-covered vine that looped around before connecting to another brand. My name had changed because I changed. That night. When I tried to kill Lucifer and showed Nathalie what I was.

I wouldn't speak my name. I hardly let myself think it, but I knew it then just like I knew it now. Much as she pissed me off, somewhere deep down, she'd left her mark on me. Permanently.

I traced the brand twice before dropping my hand. I wrapped myself in a fluffy teal-colored towel and padded down the hallway barefoot. The scent of jasmine tea and something spicy filled my nostrils as I stepped around the corner.

Nathalie looked up from whatever she was frying on the stove. "Clothes are on the bed." She thrust her head toward where I'd woken up, and I wordlessly returned to the room. Undergarments, a pair of black jeans with ribbed thighs, and a hunter green long-sleeved shirt were laid out for me. I dressed quickly, the cool air nipping at my skin. The jeans were a little tight, but workable. I shifted around, trying to loosen the material, and then pulled at the neckline of the shirt. It wasn't as high as I usually liked. The brand around my throat would be visible in it. I supposed all things considered, I couldn't complain.

Nathalie was plating food when I stepped back into the living room. She put both plates on the high bar, and then pulled out two glasses, filling them with what I could only guess was orange juice. I hadn't had it in years. It was too expensive for the budget of a bounty hunter.

"Breakfast is ready."

"I see that. . ."

I shuffled over to the counter in my too-tight jeans and peered down at the plate: real scrambled eggs, hash browns that came from an actual potato covered in spices with chunks of pepper and onion, and two slices of fresh tomato. No wonder she picked at the food from the diner when she normally got to eat this way. I took a seat at the high bar and dug in. My stomach rumbled in approval.

"So," Nathalie mused a few minutes later. "I was wondering . . ." She started. I rolled my eyes.

"Spit it out."

"What's an atma?'"

I choked on the hash browns. The spicy pepper went down the wrong pipe, and only half a glass of the best orange juice I'd ever tasted could soothe the burn and swallow it down. I wiped my mouth with the back of my hand. Nathalie wrinkled her nose.

"I have napkins, you know."

"Why do you want to know what an atma is?" I asked, ignoring her comment.

She gave me a look as if to say *are you shitting me?* I supposed that was fair.

"Two demons seem to think you're theirs, and I'm one of the only things standing between them and you—"

"I never asked you to—"

"I'm not trying to guilt you," she said sharply. "I just need the truth. You're a demon. They're demons. From context I'm assuming it's some type of weird mate bond shit. I'm asking you to help me understand."

I took a bite of tomato and chewed slowly, then swallowed.

"Mate bonds, psychic bonds, vampire brides— they are all versions of the atma bond. Trickle down from having a demon's magic," I said slowly.

She nodded. "So it's a mate bond on crack. Okay. If the other types of supernatural bonds stem from it, then I'm assuming that without completing it, both parties slowly turn feral, or in your case, all three?"

I pressed my lips together, staring hard at my plate.

"I can only assume so . . ."

She hummed under her breath. "We'll have to figure that out, then."

My chin snapped up. "You're not going to push me to go to them?"

"Not my bond, not my call—but I can't have you going feral and demoning out on me."

I narrowed my eyes at her and she chuckled. "Too soon?"

"Yes," I said stiffly. She laughed again.

We finished our breakfast, and she did the dishes before grabbing a set of keys that were hanging off a coat hook by her front door.

"All right, so here's the deal. While we're being honest with each other. I'm not staying in the cabin and neither are you." I opened my mouth to object, and she held up a hand. "Just hear me out. If we're going to find a solution to waking your sister up, we won't find it in the woods. Coming in and out of the city is risky, and there's no food out there. I'm not eating sandwiches for weeks on end."

I crossed my arms over my chest. "What do you propose, then?"

She grinned. "We stay here. My apartment is

warded, and I have a spare bedroom you can stay in, so you have more privacy. There's a food market right around the corner, and a greenhouse on the roof. We could do well here. Fix your sister. Figure out your demon problem," she mused. That was definitely one way to put it.

I mulled over her offer, taking a sweeping look of the apartment.

"I'll need to put in some added security measures—"

"Done," she agreed readily.

"No more guests," I added. She didn't so readily agree to that one.

"Barry is the only person I have over," she said, twisting the key chain on her finger.

"Don't care. No guests if Bree is going to be here. Period. You can find somewhere else to fuck—"

"It's not like that," she said quickly, her cheeks turning a shade pinker.

I grinned, and maybe it was a little cruel, but after all her poking at me, it wasn't undeserved. "Oh? Does he know that?" I lifted an eyebrow, and she narrowed her eyes.

"Fine," she said through thin lips. "No guests. Not even Barry."

She extended her pinky, and I looked at it dubiously.

"What is that?"

"A pinky promise."

"What are we five now?" I said. She dropped her hand.

"And here I thought you might like it. Break the promise and you get to break their pinky."

Well, when she put it that way, I could see the appeal.

Still, I extended my hand and we shook. A surprisingly easy truce forming. A partnership. One built on scattered trust and hard truths.

"Just remember—"

"Yeah, yeah, you'll shoot me if I betray you," she said with a wry smile.

I nodded, fighting another grin that was threatening to break through. That wouldn't do. Nope. Couldn't have her knowing that I actually liked her.

"I guess that covers it," I said.

"Come on. Grab a coat and we can head out to get your sister."

I selected a black one that was a little snug and only zipped up to my boobs. I was going to need to get more clothes. Preferably ones that fit.

We stepped out of her apartment and she locked the door behind us with a wiggle of her fingers, then muttered a spell under her breath. Symbols of protection flared on the white-paned door, then faded.

There was only one other door in the hall, other than the elevator. I eyed it as we passed. "Señora

Rosara," Nathalie said, filling in my unasked question.
We stepped into the elevator and it closed with a ding.
"She owns the shop below us and shares the greenhouse. Try not to be yourself when you meet her.
She's crotchety enough as it is." I wasn't sure exactly
what that meant. The doors opened into a place of
curiosities.

Incense burned and knickknacks lined the
shelves. Dolls that looked suspiciously like voodoo.
Orbs that glowed with bits of magic. Vials that
contained everything from toenail clippings to
eyeballs. I followed behind Nathalie as she maneu-
vered her way through aisles of junk. We were near
the door when a croak called out, "Girl, is that
you?"

"Good afternoon, Señora. This is my friend,
Piper. She'll be staying with me for a while." While
Nathalie's voice was chipper, the sour-faced woman
that stepped out from behind a hanging tapestry was
anything but.

She wore different patterns of black on her shirt
and blouse. Her hair was tied up in a makeshift
turban. She had hard brown eyes and caramel skin
that had seen better days. Giant gold hoops hung
from her ears, and every finger had at least one ring
on it.

The woman took one raking glance at me, and
said, "She looks like trouble."

"You think that about everyone," Nathalie said lightly, unoffended.

"Hmm," the old woman groused. "She gets one chance. Bring problems to my door, and I'll turn you into a cat."

As if on cue, a loud howl came from the other side of the store. A white cat darted through the front of the shop, and an even larger fat orange tabby chased after it.

I looked from the felines to the woman I was now fairly certain was a witch. She smiled in a way that left little doubt that she would do exactly as she said.

"There won't be any need for that," Nathalie said calmly. "Piper will be a model roommate. Won't you?" She directed the question at me.

"Yes," I said. The witch appraised me again.

"Mhmm. We'll see. Just remember, you'd make a fine Maine Coon if you aren't."

She turned her back and swept aside the tapestry, shuffling away.

Nathalie grabbed my arm and pulled me through the front door. A bell tinkled as we left, then rattled as a sharp wind swept by, its icy chill slapping me in the cheeks.

"Lovely neighbor you have there."

"She's an acquired taste," Nathalie said. I snorted.

"Like tequila."

She shrugged. "Señora Rosara grew up in a

different time. Her husband and son died in the
Magic Wars. It's made her a bit sharp around the
edges. Don't piss her off and she won't have a reason
to turn you into anything."

"Hmm," I hummed, not sure I was liking the idea
of staying at her apartment quite as much. Then
again, a crochety old lady was good at keeping the
vandals away. "How'd you end up living with her?"

Nathalie tucked her hands in her pockets as we
walked down the sidewalk. It was a nice day. Cold,
but not wet or cloudy. The winds were a pain, but the
sun helped warm the chill.

"I never cared for witch society. The schmoozing,
the parties, all of it. Just wasn't me. My parents
already regarded me as a failure of a daughter when
they asked me to join the Antares Coven. My condi-
tion was that I got to move out. Never specified
where. I approached Señora Rosara because she's a
hermit and they all think she's crazy." She smiled as
she recalled the memory.

"You wanted a buffer between you and your
family."

"Pretty much." She shrugged. "Besides, she's not
that bad. She likes Barry. He brings her lemon tarts
when he comes over."

I thought of the fae-witch and the way he looked
at Nathalie. I'm sure he did bring tarts to make the
old lady like him.

Nathalie came to a stop beside me and pulled out the keys. "We're still a ways from the car," I started. She hit a button, and the silver beauty beside us chirped in response.

"You can drive?" I demanded, thinking back on the conversation we had in my beat-up old Honda before we got captured by Lucifer.

"Never said I couldn't," she smirked. "You assumed, and I didn't correct you."

"I knew you were a Le Fay, but the apartment, the car—have anything else you'd like to tell me about? Maybe a hidden mansion somewhere, or a helicopter?"

Nathalie laughed as she opened the driver door. I walked around to the side and climbed in. How she had a car, and not just any car, but a nice one with a name I didn't recognize—and it wasn't damaged—was beyond me.

"No mansion or helicopters, I'm afraid. Although, my family does own a nice place in the mountains of Tennessee. It used to be a ski resort, but after the Magic Wars, business wasn't exactly booming, so they shut it down. Now they only pop in for secret coven business and stuff." She shrugged as I settled onto the leather interior. I eyed the fancy dashboard, my incredulity rising.

"So your family pays for all this?"

"I didn't say that," she replied, a bit of ice in her tone.

"Do they?"

"No," she said. "I'm independently wealthy."

I narrowed my eyes. "Independently wealthy? You? With your weird magic?"

"Yup," she said, popping the p.

"I'm not buying it," I said.

"That's nice. I'm rich, and it's my money. Whether or not you believe me is your problem." She smiled with saccharine sweetness that made me want to gag.

"I can't believe you let me pay for breakfast."

"Well, as you like to say, you're an asshole. You kidnapped me. The least you could do was buy me breakfast after leaving me tied to a chair for a day and a half and making me sick." She said it both amused and not. A tiny inkling of guilt went through me, but I pushed it down.

"I didn't know you wouldn't kill me," I pointed out.

"Mhmm," she hummed, pressing a button. The engine started, but it was only a whisper of a thing. Not the loud churn I was used to. She eased out of the spot and onto the mostly empty road.

"How do you keep this thing from getting robbed or broken into?"

She flashed me a look like I was dense. It occurred to me as she said it. "Magic."

"You don't have a cloak on it."

"Don't need one," she said, turning onto the highway. We were closer to the cabin than I realized. I'd parked further away. "I got Barry to ward it, same as the apartment."

"I don't get it," I said, leaning back and to the side. "You can do stuff like you did in the pit with Dara, and summon the wind without speaking, but you can't ward?"

Nathalie sighed. "As you like to remind me, my magic is weird. Basic spells are hard, and mine don't often work. If someone comes at me, I can defend myself. Sort of. Not even that's consistent." She shrugged.

"And the wind?" I prompted.

"I can sense it. Little threads of magic in the air. I wave my fingers and move it around harmlessly. What I did in the park and at the casino was about the extent of what I can do there."

I stared at the skyline as she drove. "You bluff an awful lot for that to be the case."

"I gotta. You know how it is. People will jack you around if they know they can. A little wiggle of my fingers, though, and most of them back off because they think I'm a lot more powerful than I am. It's when they know I'm not that I land myself in trouble." Her knuckles tightened on the steering wheel, and I couldn't tell what she was thinking, but I knew her mind had gone somewhere dark. Where they knew what she was, and she couldn't get out of it.

"You need to learn a more reliable way of keeping yourself alive," I said eventually.

"What? Like shooting?"

"If you wanted. I could teach you." I shrugged my left shoulder slightly, matching my poor attempt at offering.

Nathalie chuckled. "No offense, but you don't seem like the teaching type. I think I'll stick to bluffing while you blow everyone's brains out."

I rested my arm on the side of the door and curled it up to put the back of my hand under my chin. "That's fair. You'd probably be a shitty shot with your shaky hands."

Something whacked into my arm. I tilted my head to see Nathalie glaring at me.

"You're an asshole."

"If you're only just now realizing this, I'm going to question how smart you really are. Eidetic memory or not."

She groaned. "We're going to have to work on that too."

"What?"

"You being a dick," she muttered. I couldn't help

myself as I let out a laugh. She turned off the high-way, following the route to the cabin.

"I hate to break it to you, but that's not likely to change," I said, feeling more relaxed than I had in a long time.

"We'll see about that," she said, like I'd just issued a challenge that she had every intention of winning. The bumps of turning off pavement and onto a dirt road brought our conversation to a halt. I watched as she guided the car through the gap in the trees and all the way up to the edge of the house.

It didn't look any different than when we'd left it.

"I'm going to go grab Bree and put her in the back," I said, getting out of the car.

"Yup, you do that. I'll just sit here in the nice warm car instead of freezing my ass off," she called, half of it muffled by the sound of the door shutting.

I rolled my eyes as I climbed the steps to the cabin. I was so distracted by Nathalie that I almost didn't notice the slight crack in the door. It wasn't completely closed.

And I knew without a shadow of doubt that I had closed it when we left.

My heartbeat pulsed in my head.

My fingers brushed against the rough wood, and I pushed softly. The door swung open because it wasn't latched.

I stepped inside.

Thump. Thump. Thump.

The beat became a roar. It was the only thing that grounded me when I looked at the couch . . . because she was gone.

Bree was gone.

My legs started to work before my brain caught up. I ran at it, shoving the coffee table aside. I threw the cushions and checked the dining room and kitchen.

All the while, the word *gone* echoed in my mind, replacing the thumping sound.

I bolted down the hall and threw open the door to both the rooms and bathroom. I tore through them. I looked in the closets and under the bed like I was checking for the boogeyman. But they weren't here, and neither was she.

I went back into the living room and began to pace.

Think, I told myself. *Who could have taken her?*

Another thought entered my mind. Was it possible that after all these years, she just woke up? Did I dare hope?

"Piper," the sound of my name jerked me back to reality. I stopped pacing and turned.

The living room was destroyed, though I didn't remember doing it. I'd flipped the couch and flung the cushions everywhere. The coffee table was knocked onto its side.

Nathalie stood beside it.

In her fingers was a piece of paper.

She extended it to me wordlessly.

I took it. The way she stared at me told me that whatever was written, I wasn't going to like it.

I lowered my eyes. And then my chest squeezed, and my brands began to *burn*.

PIPER,

You told me I had to find a different way. If chasing you doesn't work, perhaps you'd rather chase me. Now that you're awake, I'll meet you at the pier in three nights' time.

Ronan

I READ the note three times before closing my fist around it. He took her. My sister. He stole her right out from under me, and I was the one that gave him the idea.

A soft touch on my shoulder made me blink. Nathalie stood in front of me.

"We'll get her back," she promised.

I nodded because that's all I could bring myself to do.

The tables had turned.

Ronan hunted me like a dog, now I would hunt him.

I may not know how to kill a demon, but I knew how to catch one.

And when I did, he was going to regret ever answering my summoning.

30

RONAN

I stood in the woods, watching her from the shadows. Piper ranted and raged, but in the end, she pressed those full lips together in grim determination and straightened her spine. Committed to hunting me down.

I knew she would.

She was a hunter, after all. Perhaps not born, but a hunter all the same.

She wouldn't be able to help herself. She would fixate on me. Obsess over every little way to get her sister back and punish me.

Little did she know, she already was.

Which is why I punished her. Well, one reason why.

I liked to watch her rage. To watch her hate. She

could be cold and indifferent to the world all she wanted, but not to me.

She was still muttering my name in contempt when she stormed out of the house and back to the car. The little witch followed behind her, then paused. Her brown eyes turned a shade of gold as she scanned the forest.

I knew the moment she saw me because—despite how well she lied—she stiffened.

I smiled cruelly at the girl and she glared back.

A tense moment passed between us.

I could sense her debating telling Piper the truth.

"Nat?" my atma called. Irritation and anger still coated her tone, though it wasn't aimed at the witch.

I lifted an eyebrow, silently asking her what she was going to do.

Her lips pressed together. She shook her head a fraction, conveying her anger. Then with a dismissive look, she turned on her heel, and called, "Nothing. Thought I saw something in the woods. It was just a squirrel."

If Piper weren't so angry, she would have noticed the way the witch's hands shook. She didn't like lying. In fact, while she could do it, she really hated doing it to Piper.

The car doors slammed shut, and gravel churned as they pulled away. I stepped through the void, into the penthouse, content with what I'd seen.

Piper would stew for the next few days.

Bree would be safe from all the supernaturals looking for ways to get their hands on Piper.

And me?

I would begin the search for Lucifer.

Piper's power should have wiped him from this existence, but somehow, he'd survived and was again hiding.

But I was going to find him.

And then, I was going to kill him.

LUCIFER

I'D BEEN WRONG.

So very wrong . . .

And now I was paying for it. Magic and fire ravaged my body, leaving me a near husk of a man. A shadow of a demon. A whisper of desire, but nothing more.

The Morningstar. The Devil. The King of the Underworld.

I'd been invincible for ten thousand years.

Until her.

A ragged cough tore through me, my chest seized, and blood splattered my form. I rolled to the side, trying and failing to reach for my magic. But where there was once a vast well of power, now only drops remained.

"Shh," Sienna said. "You need to rest. You'll never get better if you don't."

I would have responded to her, had I been able to form words. The best I could manage was grinding my teeth to keep from making any sound, because if I spoke, I would scream and howl and moan and weep.

So I chose silence.

She ran a comforting hand down my arm, and whispered, "You're burning up. I'll go grab another ice pack . . ." Her voice trailed off as she stood up from the bed. Her footsteps were quiet as they padded down the hall. I tried to focus on them, on her.

On anything but the pain.

I couldn't understand how a human could kill Aeshma. No matter how deadly or rageful or lucky. It simply shouldn't have been possible.

But now . . . now I understood.

I must have drifted off again because when the door opened, it wasn't Sienna or Sasha that spoke. In fact, it wasn't anyone I recognized at all.

"Well, well, well, look what we have here."

To be continued...

—If you loved this book, please consider reviewing on Amazon or Goodreads. I have a personal goal of trying to reach 250 reviews by Thanksgiving and it would mean so much to me if you'd drop a few lines about how you liked the book.—

Piper's story continues in:

Haunted by Shadows
Magic Wars: Demons of New Chicago
Book Two

Preorder Book 2 Here!!

ALSO BY KEL CARPENTER

Ongoing Series:

—Adult Urban Fantasy—

Demons of New Chicago:

Touched by Fire (Book One)

Haunted by Shadows (Book Two)

—Adult Reverse Harem Paranormal Romance—

A Demon's Guide to the Afterlife:

Dark Horse (Book One)

———

Completed Series:

—Young Adult +/New Adult Urban Fantasy—

The Daizlei Academy Series:

Completed Series Boxset

—Adult Reverse Harem Urban Fantasy—

Queen of the Damned Series:

Complete Series Boxset

—New Adult Urban Fantasy—

The Grimm Brotherhood Series:

Reaper's Blood (Book One)

Reaping Havoc (Book Two)

Reaper Reborn (Book Three)

—Adult Dark Fantasy—

The Dark Maji Series:

Fortune Favors the Cruel (Book One)

Blessed be the Wicked (Book Two)

Twisted is the Crown (Book Three)

For King and Corruption (Book Four)

Long Live the Soulless (Book Five)

ABOUT THE AUTHOR

Kel Carpenter is a master of werdz. When she's not reading or writing, she's traveling the world, lovingly pestering her editor, and spending time with her husband and fur-babies. She is always on the search for good tacos and the best pizza. She resides in Bethesda, MD and desperately tries to avoid the traffic.

Facebook Group
Newsletter

ACKNOWLEDGMENTS

This book is kind of special to me in a way that most of my series aren't. It's my first solo series after a long break in which I released eight co-authored books. It's also a story, like Daizlei Academy—my first series—that I strictly wrote for me.

Touched by Fire is the book I wanted to read, with romance and action and magic and post-apocalyptic vibes, but also with some deeper emotions I've been working through as a person. It was a cathartic write, and these characters are probably some of my favorites that I've ever written. I'm so very, very excited to share this book with you, and I can't wait to release more books in this world. Thank you to all of my readers that gave it a try. You guys are amazing.

Thank you to my team, for helping me perfect this

manuscript and manage all the feels. You guys helped me more than you probably even know.

And lastly, thank you to my amazing husband, who has been my rock through this crazy publishing journey that we've been on. I wouldn't be here without your cooking and never-ending support.

Made in the USA
Coppell, TX
21 November 2020

41816635R00194